GINGERBREAD AND DEADLY DREAD

MURDER ON THE MIX 4

❦

ADDISON MOORE

MURDER IN THE MIX

ADDISON MOORE

Gingerbread and Deadly Dread

BOOK DESCRIPTION

My name is Lottie Lemon, and I see dead people. Okay, so rarely do I see dead people, mostly I see furry creatures of the dearly departed variety, who have come back from the other side to warn me of their previous owner's impending doom.

That explains why I see a long-departed pooch hovering around a questionably two-timing Santa and all his naughty-hottie elves. Quite frankly, it's a terrifying sight considering the fact the fantastic phantasm is an ominous harbinger for its previous owner. So when I find my sister's boyfriend face-down in the snow with a handful of my tasty gingerbread treats, I'm not only sorry for him, but I'm very sorry that I had a blowout with him in front of the entire town of Honey Hollow. And just like that, I get the one thing for Christmas I did not ask for—a number one spot on the suspect list. I have a feeling this is going to be one Christmas I'd rather forget.

Lottie Lemon has a brand new bakery to tend to, a budding romance with perhaps one too many suitors, and she has the supernatural ability to see the dead—which are always harbingers for ominous things to come. Throw in the occasional ghost of the human variety, a string of murders, and her insatiable thirst for justice, and you'll have more chaos than you know what to do with.

Living in the small town of Honey Hollow can be murder.

CHAPTER 1

I see dead people.

Mostly I see those of the furry dearly departed variety, but last month I saw a bona fide once-upon-a human. It was my good friend Everett's father, and he, like his dearly departed predecessors, was here to warn of some unfortunate soul's impending doom. But at the moment, I'm not looking at the dearly departed—unless I can quickly arrange otherwise, and, my goodness, how I would love to—I'm staring at the perverse louse my mother has just introduced me to as her questionable date for the evening.

"*Brad Rutherford?*" I balk. "Mother, you can't be serious." My mother, Miranda Lemon, has been instilling confidence and independence in her three daughters, not to mention leading by example once my father died of a heart attack by running a successful B&B and chartering many groups that cater to women right here in Honey Hollow. Dating a well-documented philanderer who has a craving for all things kinky is taking about ten severe paces back—not just as far as her daughters are concerned, for all womankind.

Mr. Rutherford laughs as if I had fashioned those words to get a chuckle out of him. He's the cad that was cheating on his wife with Collette Jenner—the same Collette Jenner that his wife poisoned inadvertently instead of shoving this perverted oaf off to the great majority. He's a tall, stocky man with gray hair and eyes that twinkle with mischief. And I wasn't kidding about the perverse part either. It turns out, he and Collette shared a penchant for particular tastes in the bedroom, and don't get me started on the crowd they invited to participate or those kinky rough and rowdy dealings down in a seedy place called the Jungle Room. Miranda Lemon has not had great taste in men since the passing of my father, but this time she has crossed one big, fat perverted line.

"Lottie Lemon!" Mom hisses as she pulls Mr. Rutherford closer to her as if the physical proximity alone was made to drive a point home. "Please mind your manners." She wrinkles her nose and giggles. "And when you have a chance, see to it that a platter of those fabulous Christmas tree crunchies make their way to our table." They start to take off and she backtracks. "Ooh, I almost forgot to mention. There's been a rash of package thefts all over town. Please be careful. It's such a risk purchasing gifts off the internet this time of year. Pass the word around!" She gives a quick wiggle of the fingers as they take off into the crowded hall of the community center.

It's the night of the Parks and Recs Christmas extravaganza, and Lainey's two-timing boyfriend extended an invite to my mother and apparently to her two-timing date. There's a theme that I refuse to acknowledge taking place among the Lemon women—myself and my sister Meg excluded.

Tanner Redwood is the second two-timing louse of the night who makes my blood boil. I've caught him on a couple of occasions entertaining women—mostly girls who look suspiciously underage—behind my sister's back.

I choose to ignore my mother's plea for cookies at the moment, and instead make my way to the brand new refrigerated van that Everett surprised me with on Thanksgiving. Everett felt bad that I didn't win one of these beauties in the pie bake-off last month. Instead, I let my pies burn to a crisp while I helped apprehend the person responsible for Collette's death.

It's true. Everett was the only reason I was so wrapped up in the case. Essex Everett Baxter has quickly become my dear friend, so of course I wanted to help clear his good name. I met Everett in September when my old landlords took me to small claims court. Everett was the presiding judge and, well, let's just say we had a rather salacious meet and greet just prior to winding up in the courtroom together.

Speaking of salacious meet and greets—a goofy grin rides high on my face as I head out into the frozen night—my new boyfriend Noah and I sort of had a memorable meet and greet of our own on that very same afternoon. But never mind the past. Noah and I are about to venture into far more memorable waters later tonight.

The parking lot is filled to capacity as I venture into the frozen, starless night. The evergreens have cast their sensory spell on the night, loosening their oils in a rich, earthy perfume. I could inhale this scent for days. But Mother Nature hasn't forgotten about offering us a visual feast. The snow may have been cleared from the roadways, but mounds of glistening fresh powder blankets the rest of Honey Hollow. A storm just blanketed the entire town in over a foot of frosted glory, and we're well on our way to having a gorgeous white Christmas.

It's the beginning of December and already all of Main Street has been strung with white twinkle lights and huge furry wreaths punctuated with cherry red bows. The official Honey Hollow tree lighting ceremony is coming up in a few days, and the mayor himself asked me to provide the sweet treats for the occasion. Not to mention the fact the owners of the Jolly Holly Tree Lot have ordered a steady stream of holiday cookies for their staff and customers. Those are both big ticket catering events I was asked to cover this month. But the pièce de résistance is the annual community Christmas party being held at the Evergreen Manor. I've never been in charge of so many holiday desserts, but seeing that it's the first Christmas for the Cutie Pie Bakery and Cakery, I'm determined to knock it out of the park.

Suffice it to say, business is booming. There's already an order list for Christmas Eve pies as long as my arm. And as soon as we put up the gingerbread house as a part of our holiday display, we've been baking and assembling the cute, candied cottages at breakneck pace—it seems every customer wants at least two. And that fact alone is the very reason the entire bakery, all of Main Street just outside our doors—and I'd venture to say the entire great state of Vermont holds the spiced scent of ginger and black strap molasses. It's a lovely combination that I can't seem to get enough of this time of year, which is exactly why I baked three times as many gingerbread cookies as I did those Christmas tree crunchies my mother can't seem to get enough of.

A car pulls up next to me and out steps a dapper looking Essex Everett Baxter, the aforementioned honorable judge who happens to be my new next-door neighbor as well. Everett is tall, commanding in every sexual way, and, dare I say, handsome to a fault. He's not one to smile easily. The sound of his laughter is a rare treat, and he manages to garner the attention of every female in a five-mile radius with all that raw testosterone he oozes.

"Lemon"—he nods my way before holding out his hands, and I give him two foil-covered platters to carry in—"you look spectacular this evening." He says it with a note of suspicion as his eyes do that broken elevator thing up and down my body. Everett and I happen to share a special bond because he just so happened to wrangle my supernatural secret out of me last month. Up until then only Nell Sawyer, my BFF's Grammy, knew anything about the fact I can see the dead. Believe you me, I wasn't hungry to tell Everett, and a small part of me still resents how insistent he was that I tell him. Those threats to go to the police didn't help either. But now that the dearly departed cat is out of the bag, I feel comfortable knowing my secret is safe with him. I feel terrible that Everett is privy to something that Noah is not. But my new boyfriend has nothing to worry about. I'm about to make him privy to a whole lot more of me in just a few hours.

Noah is tall, dark, and handsome as well, but not in any conventional sense. His dark hair is thick and glossy, the color of a raven's wing. And when it hits the light, it catches fire and makes my insides dissolve with lust. Those marbled verdant green eyes of his remind me of the rich pine trees that Honey Hollow seems to be comprised of. And when he looks right at me, I have a distinct feeling I should yank him into the nearest broom closet and have my way with him. His cheeks are peppered with permanent stubble, and every time he's around my fingers twitch to touch him. Noah is irresistibly sexy, and that would explain the fact women seem to lean in whenever he's around. That arresting amount of testosterone he's been gifted naturally acts as a gravitational pull. He, much like Everett, is slow to smile. Bedroom eyes seem to be his default, and he just so happens to be Ashford County's number one homicide detective.

Some might contest that last fact, but I happen to know it's the truth.

"Earth to Lottie." Everett ducks down to my height a moment. "I said you look stunning. You really dressed to the nines."

My cheeks heat to unsafe levels. "Yes, well, it is a special night. I hear there's a talent show we'll be treated to, and let's not forget it's the first holiday party of the season."

"For the Parks and Recs Department." He continues with his wary scrutinizing stare. "You look like you're about to head off to prom."

I cringe at the high school-esque analogy. "Is it that obvious?" I glance down at the emerald gown—strapless no less, with a matching velvet shawl pinned together with an old rhinestone brooch in the shape of a candy cane—my biggest and best find at Goodwill this month. I had to eschew the heels for my warm, cozy winter boots, but that's because I'm still on duty and heels are simply not practical while working with baked goods in any capacity.

I'm not usually one to dress to the nines for any occasion, for sure not when it means my bones will be so cold they'll threaten to shatter the way they are now, but Noah and I decided this was the night we would exchange holiday gifts a little early.

We've decided to give the gift that keeps on giving—each other. So understandably I wanted to look like a stunning woman, not a teenager who has heavily abused her cosmetic privileges. Although, in my defense, I logged about a thousand makeup tutorials to get my contouring and highlighting just right to avoid the aforementioned high school malfeasance. Not only did I plunk down a decent amount of change at the beauty counter for all the Spackle that went into the making of this disaster piece, but it took me three hours to achieve the *natural* look.

"Never you mind what I'm up to. You look rather dapper

yourself." I happen to know he's just left work. Everett leaves the house and comes home every single day in a three-piece suit with a dark wool coat thrown over it, and that's exactly what he has on now. "You came for my cookies, didn't you?"

He smacks his lips as he looks to the bustling community center before us. "That and the fact Lily extended the invite."

"Working on another ex, I see." I'd rather gag myself with a candy cane or poke my eyes out with an evergreen bough than witness Lily Swanson cavorting with Everett. Lily works for me at the bakery, and she's also the BFF of my long-time self-professed nemesis, Naomi Turner—who happens to be the twin of my own BFF, the fabulous Keelie Turner. Keelie runs the Honey Pot Diner, which is the adjoining establishment to the Cutie Pie. Her Grammy Nell owns both.

Everett rumbles with a dull laugh. "Can one ever have enough?"

"Most people can—with me at the top of the list. Noah and I are forever." I can't help but beam as I say it. Noah and Everett used to be stepbrothers back when they were in high school. I'm not quite sure how they truly feel about one another now, but they seem tolerant to say the least.

Keelie bounces in our path just as we enter the back door to the kitchen. "I come bearing gifts!" She holds up a sparkly tote in the shape of a hot pink Christmas stocking. Keelie Turner is as bubbly and cute as her name suggests with her blonde curls bouncing around her shoulders and her blue eyes gleaming with wicked intent. "Look!" She plucks the gift from the bowels of the hot pink stocking and shakes out something red with frilly white trim that looks as soft as down feathers. It's not until she holds it up, with two hands for Everett and me to inspect, do I wheeze with embarrassment.

"Keelie Nell Turner!" I shout as I do my best to snatch the raunchy accouterment from her hot little hands.

"What?" She cackles into the night as Everett and I make our way past her. "Tonight's the perfect night for you to dress up as a naughty Mrs. Claus."

Everett lifts a brow my way as we set down our platters.

"Is that why you're dressed to impress, Lemon? It's prom night for Noah and you?"

I give a quick glance at the kitchen staff before smacking Everett on the arm. "Would you keep it down? It is not prom night for Noah and me. I refuse to liken what's about to take place to some high school sexual blunder filled with teen angst and regret."

Keelie steals a peppermint melt-away and moans as she takes a bite. She's dressed head to toe as Santa's naughty little elf in a tight sequin dress that hardly covers her rear, red and white striped tights, and a pair of high-heeled boots with the toes curling upwards like red satin snakes, each one tipped with a tiny silver bell.

"I'd better get back out there," she mumbles with a mouthful. "Tanner's break is just about up, and Lord knows he needs me to hold back those *ho ho hos* from stampeding his throne. He's quite the holiday rock star."

"He's quite the holiday as—"

"Lemon," Everett presses it out with a hint of judgment—his specialty might I add.

"I was going to say astonishment."

No sooner does Keelie take off than a beautiful strawberry blonde Golden Retriever bounds right in through the back door and gets trapped between me and the pantry.

"Oh my goodness! Well, look at you!" I say, bending over and tousling its soft flurry fur. "Someone is going to be very sorry they let you out of their sight and on a night like tonight! You could freeze to death out there."

It nuzzles against my hand, and I feel a collar and a nametag.

Just as I gently pull it forward to get a look at it, the sweet beast tips its head up, revealing eyes that burn red with fire.

"*Gah!*" I jump back and straighten, only to meet with a less than amused look on Everett's face.

His eyes widen a notch. "You see another one, don't you?"

My mouth opens a moment as I ponder my options, but unfortunately for me, the truth wins out.

"Yes, Everett, I do."

It turns out, this beautiful phantasm of a beast wasn't about to freeze to death after all.

But I'm guessing someone at the community center is in store for more than just a holly jolly evening.

They're about to get a permanent ride to the other side, courtesy of the Grim Reaper's jingle bell express.

CHAPTER 2

The Honey Hollow Community Center is filled to the brim with bodies as the Parks and Rec holiday jubilee gets ready to kick off. The entire room is festooned with garland and wreathes made of fresh evergreen branches giving it that earthy pine scent that makes my spirit sing. There's enough mistletoe hung in every nook and cranny to raise the heat level of the room another fifty degrees, and the twinkle lights strewn across the ceiling make it look as if we're celebrating under the stars.

The event itself is open to all of the Parks and Recs Departments of Ashford County, so that encompasses Honey Hollow,

Hollyhock, and Leeds as well. Of course, everyone was encouraged to bring family or a plus one—and for a small donation, anyone else is welcome to join in. Aside from refreshments and my sweet desserts, the Honey Pot Diner brought a four-course holiday feast to please even the most finicky palate. All of this is on the county dime, of course. With so many cutbacks, it's nice to see that there's still enough left to bankroll a good old-fashioned Christmas party.

I spot my sister Lainey toward the entrance, craning her neck frantically every which way, probably looking for Tanner, the twit she never should have ended up with. Even though the Lemon family adopted me as an infant, Lainey and I still share the same long caramel waves and light hazel-green eyes.

I want so much better for my sister than Tanner Redwood. Lainey and her long-time true love, Forest Donovan, had a nasty falling-out last summer and, well, that disaster still hasn't rectified itself.

Just as I'm about to flag her down, Everett grabs ahold of my elbow and speeds us down the corridor in the back.

"Lemon, we need to discuss this."

"Would you let go? I'm going to drop my goodies!" I grabbed a platter of my to die for gingerbread cookies on our way out of the kitchen. The staff will be serving up the rest of the treats I've brought for the celebration, but I always like to offer up a round of my delectable delights myself just to see those wide grins break out once people take a bite. "There's nothing to discuss." I glance past him as that adorable Golden Retriever with those menacing red eyes bounds in and out of the crowd.

"Call Noah," he insists. "Call every sheriff's department in the country. Call the fire department, the FBI, the CIA—"

"No," I say sternly, my finger rising to his chest. "I can't just alert the authorities. What am I supposed to say? Excuse me, I see the ghost of the cutest Golden Retriever that ever lived, and I'm pretty sure a homicide is about to take place?"

Those deep blue eyes of his bulge for a moment. "Yes. *No.* I don't know. Maybe." He rakes his fingers through his hair.

The sound of shrill wheezing comes from behind, and I step around a couple of discarded boxes only to find a young girl with her hands discreetly hidden in—oh my Honey Hollow stars, are those Santa's pants?

"*Tanner!*" I bark so loud that the girl dismounts ungracefully and makes a run for it. The only thing I can make out clearly is her scarlet hair bouncing like flames.

"Excuse me," Tanner huffs as he pushes past us on his way back into the main hall while doing his best to adjust that ridiculous velour suit he's stuffed himself into.

"Did you see that?" I squawk to Everett. "That was no saint. That was Tanner Redwood disgracing the good name of Santas everywhere while openly cheating on my sister!"

Everett winces. "He wasn't exactly doing it in the open."

"Do *not* defend him!" My phone bleats, and I pluck it out of my purse. "It's a text from Noah." My cheeks flush with heat at the thought of seeing him—*all* of him in a few short hours. I read the text and bite down over my bottom lip to keep from grinning like an idiot. "He says he's finishing up early, and he'll be here soon."

"Not soon enough. Let's get back out there and see if we can find out who might need our help."

I tug him back by the sleeve of his coat, a laugh caught in my throat. "Our help?"

"Yes. I'm not letting you go out there on your own while there's a murderer on the loose."

"We don't know that."

"It's a darn good guess."

Everett and I head into the thicket of bodies heating the

community center to sweltering degrees. There's no sign of that fuzzy, cute, all too excitable retriever, but I do spot Lainey standing less than a few feet away, her arm threaded with that unsavory Santa as he regales a small crowd of co-workers with his false persona. Apparently, he's been honing his skills on my sister all these months. I can't wait to tell Lainey all about that tacky tryst Everett and I just witnessed.

I haul Everett over with me, and Lainey beams at the sight of us.

"I'm so glad you made it! And you brought a date." She gives a hearty wink.

Very funny. Lainey knows Everett and I are just friends. She also knows that after dropping off the cookies for the event I was about to hightail it out of here and finish decorating my home for Noah and me with candles and pizza—the pizza was less for decorating purposes and more a staple I was securing to maintain our stamina. I've already ordered three extra-large with everything on them from our favorite Italian restaurant Mangia. One for all three days we've marked off to enjoy our carnal feast. This weekend will mark the very first days off I've had from the Cutie Pie Bakery since it's been in operation. It's going to feel odd, terrifying, *irresponsible* as if I've accidentally left a toddler unsupervised at the mall.

Tanner belts out a hearty *ho ho ho* and the small crowd huddled around us chortles with delight.

Lainey lifts a hand my way. "Everyone, this is my sister Lottie and her good friend Everett. Lottie, Everett, this is, well —*everyone!*"

"Hello!" I sing as I quickly offer them each an adorable gingerbread cookie complete with humble smiles and miniature red Santa hats iced over their foreheads. They really are the cutest batch I've whipped up in ages. Tanner helps himself to a fistful, and I can't help but scowl. Even dressed as the man in red he has absolutely zero decorum. But I've known that about him for a good long while now. Chrissy Nash is the only familiar face to me in this small circle. She's the mayor's ex, and if I'm not mistaken, he's roving the premises, too. I can't imagine what it would be like to constantly run in the same social circles as your cheating ex-husband.

A tall, lantern-jawed man steps our way. He's got one of those charming twirly old-timey mustaches that lends itself to an era long gone by, eyes that smile all on their own, and is that a—

"*Gah!*" I squeal while jumping behind Everett and employing him as a human shield. The small crowd around us lights up with laughter once again, this time on my behalf.

Sitting on the mustache man's arm is one of those ultra-creepy wooden dummies with the face of an over-animated child. It's only then I note they're both dressed in matching gray checkered suits, making the dummy look like some bizarre extension of the man himself.

"Hello!" The dummy's mouth opens and closes, and its eyes give a clumsy blink. "My name is Darjeeling, and this here dummy is Ned Sweeny," the doll chatters the words out with the clattering of its fake wooden teeth.

"Clever," I say since I seem to be the victim of this monster's depravity.

The man, Ned Sweeny, I presume, belts out a laugh. "You look scared to death! Don't worry. He won't get you." He lifts the piece of fabric from the dummy's back. "I've got about twenty of these to match my suits. It's an extra coattail that attaches with Velcro and gives us a seamless appeal. I find it less distracting. That way people can focus on Darjeeling and not where he ends and I begin."

"Lovely," I say, looking to Everett who's busy glaring at the wooden demon.

"We'll be performing in just a bit," Darjeeling reassures us with a click of his teeth. "Prepare to be annoyed by the tall, stiff one." The dummy leans in, glancing over his shoulder as if he's about to divulge a secret. "He's got a real wooden personality, if you know what I mean."

Our small circle warms with laughter once again, but the young girl by his side, dressed in a long red cape, rolls her eyes as if she's had enough of the show already—and, believe you me, I'm with her. Cute cape though. I'll have to ask where she bought it. I'm just about to extend a compliment when a long scarlet tendril falls to her shoulder.

I suck in a quick breath. It's her! The trollop I found crawling all over Santa's lap just a few minutes ago. I shoot Lainey a knowing look and tip my head toward the scarlet sleaze ball—not that it's entirely Red Riding Hood's fault, but surely my sister must suspect something.

A brunette with a pixie cut and enormous silver hoop earrings—my goodness, I think they were intended to be bracelets—clears her throat.

"I for one am looking forward to the show and then some." She offers a flirtatious wink to the three-foot wooden creature as if it were real. "I happen to have a soft spot for men without a brain."

Explosive laughter breaks out, and Darjeeling, the creepiest entity in the room—and considering there's a fiery-eyed phantasm floating around says a lot—laughs right along with us before leaning her way.

"Then you'll love this guy!" He jerks his head toward his twisted owner.

"Sorry, ladies"—Ned Sweeny, the man himself, speaks up in a much deeper octave than he allows his sidekick—"but I've got a wife and two kids. I'm taken."

More laughter ensues, and this time it's me rolling my eyes up at Everett. I'm betting he's sorry Lily Swanson ever wrangled him into this questionably good time.

Our circle begins to break up, and a man near Tanner leans in and whispers something into his ear. I can't help but note that the young man reminds me a bit of Noah with the same dark hair with red highlights, chiseled features, and broad shoulders.

"It's almost show time!" someone cries from the stage, and my entire body bucks.

It's almost show time indeed. The sooner Noah gets here, the sooner we can get out of here.

"Dude." Tanner ticks his head back, shooting the Noah looka-like the stink eye.

He would.

And then, without a warning, Tanner nods over to someone and starts to take off. "Be back in five, babe!" He shoots my sister with his finger. So not a Santa move.

Is it really too much to ask of him to stay in character while in that suit? There are children present, for Pete's sake. And I have it on good authority that Santa does not say *dude*.

No sooner does Tanner ditch us than *Little Red Riding Ho* follows right after him.

"That's it!" I say, snatching Lainey by the wrist. "What you're about to witness is going to be upsetting, and even though you won't think this is the time or the place, you'll thank me come morning. And on a bright note, it also happens to be your get-out-of-ventriloquist-hell free card because I'll bet good money neither you nor I will want to stick around for the scary show." I yank her along with me toward the infamous corridor where I'm sure Santa is looking to offer a quickie sleigh ride to that less than sweet tart.

"Where are you taking me?" Lainey does her best to yank free.

Everett strides by my side. "You see him, don't you, Lemon?" He's all eyes as he scans the vicinity. Come to think of it, Everett would make one hot G-man. If the feds are looking for a few good men, they'd be lucky to have him.

"I sure will in one hot-to-trot second." No sooner do the words speed out of me than I realize Everett probably meant our loyal friend from the great beyond. This is really panning out to be a spooktacular Christmas party after all.

"Would you stop! You're choking the life out of my fingers!" my sister shrills her nonstop protest in my ear as we speed to that tower of boxes, and no sooner do we turn the corner than we spot the salacious Santa with a girl wrapped around his waist like a flesh-colored serpent.

"Tanner Redwood!" Lainey roars like the bloodthirsty lioness I always knew she could be. "You are a dead man!" she shrieks so loud the corridor fills with an unexpected crowd.

The girl ambles down and bolts, but not before I note those oversized hoop earrings jostling from side to side. It's her! The girl who said she liked men without a brain. Boy, she wasn't kidding. And shockingly, Tanner here might just be overqualified for the position. His lack of brain cells goes above and beyond the call of duty.

Lainey proceeds to pummel him as Everett and I do our best to pluck her off the red-suited jackass.

"Let me at him!" Lainey howls as we struggle to hoist her away, and Tanner the two-timer bolts down the hall and out the back door presumably to safety. Not if my sister has anything to do with it.

"Let me at him!" I shout, rivaling her ferocity and fury.

"I'm going to strangle you!" she shouts after him.

"I'm going to strangle you!" My voice rises to its upper octaves.

"No, wait!" Lainey hops in the direction Tanner took off in. "Strangling you is too easy! I'm going to chop you up piece by piece and feed you to the wolves!"

I shrug over at Everett. "She's a librarian. She loves to read. It really does give her a great imagination."

"I can't believe this!" Lainey shakes herself free from our hold on her just as another tall, handsome, heart-stopper bounds our way.

"Forest!" My entire affect brightens. As bad as I feel for making her witness what she did, it warms my heart to see Forest showing up like a knight in shining armor—only he happens to be wearing an inky dark suit. Normally, Forest wears a suit of a different color, as in yellow. He loves Lainey so much he followed in our father's footsteps and became a firefighter. My dad sure did love Forest. And I'm sure if he were here now, it would warm his heart to see him comforting his distraught daughter.

"What happened?" Forest trots past us at the void in Tanner's wake. "Did that idiot hurt you?"

"You bet he did!" Lainey riots toward the exit. "And I'm going to make sure he pays!"

"Not before I do. I'm going to kill him!" Forest takes off and ditches out the exit before we can stop him. Tanner Redwood isn't worth felony assault charges, but I'm not opposed to Forest getting a good left hook in after the way he treated my sister.

"Lottie!" a woman cries from the entry to the kitchen, and I turn to find a frantic Lily Swanson—Everett's official plus one for the evening. Lily is a stunner with long, dark hair that has a life of its own, a face and body that demand the attention of any and every man who seems to step into the bakery, including Everett—sans Noah, of course. "Someone just tipped over two trays of snowcapped brownies, and now we're short for the dessert table. To top it off, they want us to have a mini platter on every table by the time the show starts!"

The lights dim in the community center, and the room breaks out into hushed urgent tones as the crowd migrates to their seats.

"I'll be right there, Lily." I turn to Everett. "Get my sister to her car, and don't you dare let her out of your sight. I'll be right over once I deal with this fiasco."

I take off and, sure enough, the Gestapo running this circus is chewing out poor Lily as she cleans up the mess.

"I've got this," I say, taking the broom from her. "Go ahead and pull a few dinner plates from the pantry, and I'll help you make up the mini platters. We'll have more than enough dessert, I promise."

I head over to the broom closet to get a dustpan and note a strawberry blond tail sweeping back and forth.

A breath hitches in my throat.

"No, no, not tonight," I mutter to myself as I find the fantastic phantasm desperately trying to lap up one of my snowcapped brownies from off the floor to no avail. "Hey there," I say, running my fingers gently over his luxurious coat, and he quickly rolls onto his back until I'm scratching his belly. "You like this, don't you?" I can't help but laugh. He's such a beautiful, noble beast, and at the moment he looks to be smiling with his tongue hanging to the side, his left leg thumping a mile minute. "That's your spot, isn't it?" I say, increasing the velocity. It never ceases to amaze me at how real they feel to me. They might be shy of one carnal body, but they sure look and feel like the real deal.

It looks up at me with those glowing red eyes and whimpers as if trying its best to lick up the mess once again.

"I'm sorry you can't indulge. But if it makes you feel any better, brownies have far too much chocolate in them and they could kill you." I wince as I say it. I suppose it's rather a moot point anyway. "In that case, I'd sweep up both platters and let you have at it, but as fate and your lack of a digestive system would have it, I guess I have to clean the mess up myself." A silver charm dangles from his neck. "I bet I can find out who you belonged to. Maybe there's a number on here?" I balk at the thought. Like I'm really going to call someone and say you'd better watch your back. There's a good chance you might be slaughtered in your sleep tonight. That would go over real well. But there's no number, just the name *Dutch* written across the front.

"Dutch?"

As soon as I say it, his head jerks up—and he is indeed a boy. I gleaned that fact a moment ago while he was rolling around getting his tummy scratched to his heart's content.

Dutch sits up straight as if he heard someone calling his name from a distance, those fiery eyes pinned on something behind me. Then, just like that, he takes off and runs out the back door that leads to the parking lot.

"Hey!" I call out, abandoning the broom as I speed into the night after him. I follow his golden fur through the lot and up a small mound of snow and stop short at the sight of something red sprawled out before me about twenty yards away. Sitting dutifully by that pile of cheap red velour and curly white wig is that red-eyed retriever.

It takes all of my strength to hustle my way over, my boots sinking into the powder well past my ankles.

Lying facedown in the snow is Tanner Redwood with one of my gingerbread cookies still curled in his hand. There's a foot-long icicle piercing the side of his neck, and I quickly fall to my knees and pluck it out.

"*Lottie?*" a familiar voice booms from behind as Noah races his way over, a bouquet of red roses in his hand, the other on his gun. "What the heck is going on?"

"It's Tanner," I pant. "He's dead."

CHAPTER 3

There have been times in my life when I have really regretted leaving my bed in the morning. There have been places I've been to that I wish I could retrace my steps and erase any evidence of my presence. This moment in time happens to be a healthy mixture of both.

"I know what this looks like," I say, panting up a storm while holding a bloodied icicle over Tanner Redwood's stone-cold body.

"Did you kill him, Lottie?" The flowers slip from Noah's hand as he staggers over and does a quick check of Tanner's pulse.

"No," I say, dropping the murderous weapon and struggling to get back on my feet as the snow does its best to hold me still as if it were placing me under arrest itself. "I found him. I was in the kitchen, and there was this dog." I come close to covering my mouth before noting the pink stain on my frozen fingers. "Anyway, I came out and found him like this, and then you showed up."

Noah is already on his phone calling in a possible homicide, and my stomach churns just hearing it.

No sooner does the phone call end than the howl of sirens saw through the night.

"Lottie"—Noah wraps an arm around me, gently pushing the hair from my face—"did you see anything at all? Did you notice anything funny going on inside?"

"No. I mean, yes. I caught him cheating on Lainey twice in one night. With two different women!" I can't seem to catch my breath as I say it. Every emotion under the sun is rushing through me, and as petty as it sounds, I'm still angry about the fact Tanner thought it would be acceptable to be so brazen.

"You're okay." Noah holds me while he inspects my features. My word, he's so stunningly handsome with the snow behind him, the dark sky framing him from above. Those flowers he dropped lie cold in the snow, so very stunning in their own right.

"Were those flowers for me?" My voice is lower than a whisper as if Tanner could hear.

Tanner's the only other one out here other than the loyal Golden Retriever who's lying by his side with his head resting over his paws, those glowing red eyes set to Tanner.

Noah's dimples press in deep. "Yes, Lot, they are." He lands a soft kiss to my lips. "In a second I'll get both them and you back in that warm room, but you have to tell me if you saw anything else going on with Tanner in there. Did he argue with anyone? Did anyone exhibit any threatening behavior toward him?"

Lainey's fierce reaction when she caught him red-handed comes back to me, and I shrink a little in Noah's arms.

"*Lottie?*" It almost sounds like a reprimand when he puts the inflection on my name like that.

"Fine. Lainey flipped her lid when she caught him with another woman. She may have screamed that she was going to kill him—over and over again—the screaming, not the killing." I wince. "But we both know she's innocent. Besides, I told Everett to take her to her car and wait there for me. I bet that's where she is right now."

"Lottie?" a male voice booms from behind, and we turn to see Everett jogging through the snow as he makes his way over. "Have you seen your sister?" His mouth falls open as he spots the pile of red velour and white curls. "Oh no."

"Oh yes," Noah says just as a dozen sheriff's vehicles pull into the lot.

In a moment, the entire place is swarming with deputies.

Captain Jack Turner—Keelie's father who took me under his wing after my own father passed away—calls both Noah and me over.

"Start talking." He folds his enormous arms over his belly and gives me that look that I've grown to dread. Jack is tall and stately. He has always had a calm, in-control demeanor about him that has settled my spirit, but it doesn't seem to be working at the moment.

I spill out all the details I know sans the part about the handsome retriever, or anything to do with the fact my sister was openly threatening bodily harm to the recently deceased. There are simply some things better left unspoken.

"*Lottie.*" Jack stomps his foot over the ground with great restraint. His face is quickly turning purple as if he were holding his breath. "You have got to stop stumbling upon dead bodies. This is beyond reasonable at this point."

"But I was never responsible before as I'm not now. *And* I've always graciously helped you catch the killer." Dear Lord, it's like I've been cursed to magnetize to the dead. Those pesky polter-geists don't exactly help my dilemma either.

Noah groans at the thought. He's not exactly enthused over the fact I've infused myself into any of the aforementioned investigations. In fact, it's often a point of contention between us.

"I'm here!" a husky female calls out as none other than detec-tive Ivy Fairbanks jogs up to the scene. "A deputy just briefed me." She flits her luminescent eyes to mine. "I understand you were at the scene of the crime—again." A paper white fog plumes from her mouth and gives her the appeal of a dragon. I've always suspected she's had serpentine roots.

Ivy is a redheaded beauty with a mean streak a mile wide. She's tall and stately and carries herself with enough confidence to let you know she's not afraid of anything, namely me. Although, she might scare me just a bit. A fact I'm not proud of.

Jack turns to me. "Excuse us, Lottie." The three of them shuffle off to the side just as my sister clip-clops out into the parking lot in her four-inch stilettos. My sister has never been one to eschew fashion because of a little snow on the ground.

"Careful, you're going to slip." I trot over with my arms set wide as if I had the power to catch her from three feet away. "Where were you? And please, dear Lord, let there have been witnesses!"

"What? I was in the bathroom bawling my eyes out when I wasn't screaming out obscenities."

"The bathroom! That's perfect! I bet half the community center saw you head on in."

"I doubt it. Once I ditched Everett, I took off for the one in the foyer. Hot tip: it's dead out there. Not a single line in the ladies' room. Not a soul in sight." She wrinkles her nose past my shoulder. "What's going on out there? I was just coming to get you. There seems to be a problem with the show."

"It's pretty much dead out there, too." I grip my sister by the shoulders. "Brace yourself, Lainey. This is *not* good news."

"Oh my word, Forest!" Her voice riots into the night and miraculously Forest Donovan appears from nowhere and wraps his arms around her as if she just summoned him from the great beyond. They exchange a quick, and might I add heated, embrace before Lainey turns back to me. "If it's not Forest, who is it?"

"You didn't hear?" Forest runs his finger under her jawline, and it looks tender and intimate as if they never skipped a beat. "They found Tanner. He's dead."

"*What?*" Lainey's eyes blow up the size of my cookie platters. "Oh my goodness, they think I did it, don't they? Wait—was he butchered to death just the way I pictured? Oh good grief, I'm an animal! I have the superpower to kill by way of suggestion!"

Forest drums out a sorrowful laugh as he struggles to get her attention once again. "I promise, you're in the clear."

Jack Turner comes up with his badge shining under the streetlamp. "Lottie—Lainey Lemon? I'd like to have a word with you girls. Witnesses say you were having a fit with the deceased just a few minutes before *you*"—he glowers at me a moment— "were found hovering over his body with an icicle."

Lainey gasps just as Forest averts his eyes.

"I didn't do it, I swear. I found him in the snow, and I plucked that thing out of his neck. I thought I might save his life. You don't think this has anything to do with those package thefts, do you?" Silly, I know, but right about now, I'd say anything to take the spotlight off of me.

Poor Jack's eyes double in size. "No, Lottie, I don't."

Ivy Fairbanks struts up with an unreasonably handsome Noah by her side. It is so not fair that he only gets better looking as the night wears on. This night of all nights.

"We'll take it from here, captain." Ivy strides over, looking every bit the supermodel she secretly is. "Lottie, we have your prints on file at the station. We'll still need to question you both at length." She looks to Forest. "You as well, Donovan. Witnesses saw you running out the back."

I glance over my shoulder and, sure enough, every person who was in the community center has created a ring outside of the barrier the sheriff's department has erected.

Ivy separates Lainey and me, and I watch as both my sister and Forest take off with Noah.

"I suppose it was too much to ask to have my boyfriend conduct the questioning."

Ivy smirks at the thought. "Boyfriend? How very junior high of you."

"Is not," I'm quick to protest as she ticks her head for me to follow her over to an opened police cruiser. "It's perfectly acceptable for a woman of any age to refer to her love interest as a boyfriend. It sure sounds a lot better than gentleman caller. Now *that* sounds all kinds of wrong."

She practically shoves me into the back seat while hovering intimidatingly over me with a notepad in hand while I lob answers at all the asinine questions she tosses my way. Again, I cleverly leave out both that cute little golden pooch and my sister's tirade. Ivy here is going to have to do more than dance for her dinner if she ever expects to get anything so juicy out of me.

She slips her pen against the notebook before looking back to the community center. "I've got an entire fleet of people to speak with before the night is through. You're free to go. Don't leave town. I might make a pit stop at that bakery of yours."

"Sounds great. I look forward to your visit." I'm sure it's not a sin at all to lie to an authority on the night a beautiful pooch leads you to a dead body.

A happy yelp comes from the field, and I look over to see the beautiful beast illuminated from the inside with a golden glow as he bounds his way over with a joyful bark.

"I can hear you!" I marvel as he skips his way over, and I give his neck a quick pat. Those flaming red eyes of his don't look half as scary now that I've gotten to know him a bit. Then it hits me. *Gah!* I heard him! I heard him bark. I can *hear* his panting.

Oh my dear Lord up in heaven, forgive me. It's never gone this far before. It's never at all been vocal. Come to think of it, I heard him back in the kitchen whimpering over the brownies he couldn't eat. Not even Everett's father who graced us with his ghostly presence was of the verbal variety.

Hey? I wonder if this means my powers are getting stronger?

Powers. I hate that word. But in all honesty, I have never known how to frame this strange yet spooky ability of mine.

Ivy glances back at me with disdain. "Yes, you heard me." She sniffs as her gaze drops to the friendly pup as if she could see him. "What are you doing?"

"Oh!" My fingers quickly migrate to my shin. "I have an itch. Probably fleas. I've got plenty of those."

"Fleas? This time of year?"

Before I can answer, Noah crops up behind her, and Ivy offers him a wry smile.

"I'd look out if I were you, Detective Fox. Your little girlfriend has fleas." She takes off as I struggle to come up with a clever response.

"Don't you listen to her." I wrap my arms around Noah as his chest rumbles with a dull laugh. "For one, I don't have fleas. And two, I'm not that little. That's just her way of being condescending."

"I'm not listening to her, I promise." He bounces his nose to mine. "At least regarding the fleas. Unfortunately, as my superior, I do have to obey her authority, and it looks as if I have not only a very long night ahead of me but a very long weekend." A pained expression takes over as he lifts a cautious brow. "I'm sorry."

"You're sorry? I'm fit to kill." I bite down over my lip. "I guess we'll have to postpone our plans." I scour the lot a moment. "Hey? Where's my sister?"

"Forest took her to Ashford. She's pretty shaken up. We're taking their prints, Lottie. Just basic stuff. No need to panic. He mentioned he'd get her home and stay the night."

"Staying the night? I've gone from feeling sorry for my sister to envying her." I give his ribs a quick pinch, and a momentary smile bounces on his lips.

Figures. Noah and I move heaven and earth to make sure we get three blissful days together, and, it turns out, all the coital luck goes to Lainey and Forest. Although, I seriously doubt anything of the coital variety will be happening for the two of them on a night like tonight. If I were them, I'd settle for a few good, hearty embraces and maybe an entire slew of I'm sorrys. At least it's a start.

A horrible moan comes from me as Dutch stirs at my feet. "I can't believe this is happening, and on this Friday night of all Fridays. It's horrible all around. I'm sorry for Tanner, and I'm sorry for us, too. Rain check?"

"I promise."

"At least I've got the flowers." I glance over and find them firmly within the bounds of the bright yellow caution tape. The sheriff's department just set up a spotlight over the scene as the coroner's van rolls lazily into the lot. A mean shiver runs though me at the sight. I don't think there's a person on the planet who can ever get used to that sight, with the exception of the coroner, of course.

"About that..."

"I don't have flowers anymore, do I?"

"They were a little too close to the body. The captain thinks they should be carefully exhumed in the event they're covering evidence. But you will have flowers. New, better flowers." He drops a warm kiss over my lips, and it's as if all of Honey Hollow melts away for a moment. Noah's kisses have always held a world of magic to them. "You will have lots and lots of flowers."

I shake my head up at him. "Those were more than enough. I just want you."

His dimples dig in a moment, no smile, as his mouth takes mine. Noah blesses me with a bone-shattering kiss that makes me want to kidnap him from the scene and take him to another state entirely. But I don't. Instead, I let him walk me to my car, and shockingly Dutch, the ever-faithful retriever, hops right in, too.

We take off for home, just my newly acquired spectral with the glowing red eyes and me.

Not exactly how I envisioned this evening would end. I just hope to high heaven my sweet Himalayan, Pancake, doesn't share my gift for all things supernatural. Things could get dicey.

I look in my rearview mirror as those red and blue lights continue to spasm into the night.

Things are already dicey.

That frozen spear I plucked from him comes to mind, and I look down over my fingers, still stained pink with Tanner Redwood's blood.

Someone killed Tanner, and I know for a fact it wasn't Forest, Lainey, or me.

Well, I know for a fact it wasn't Lainey and me.

A dull groan evicts from my throat.

I know for a fact it wasn't me. And that doesn't make me feel a whole lot better.

Both Forest and Lainey were angry enough to do it.

But are they killers?

I suppose I'll have to find out.

CHAPTER 4

t turns out, Pancake can in fact detect the golden malfeasance I've brought home with me.

"*Rawrr!*" The butter yellow hair on the back of his neck stands up on end as he runs from one corner of the room to the next, and bounding behind him like a living, breathing, demon-eyed cutie is Dutch in full-on attack mode.

"Stop!" I scream as Dutch and those blazing red eyes chase Pancake around the room, nearly knocking over my end table and sending my ginger jar lamp wobbling on its base. "*Gah!*" I do my best to right it just as a knock erupts on the door.

"Just a minute!" I sing just as Pancake whizzes by, and I make an effort to flop on top of him—stopping just shy of turning Pancake into a, well, a pancake. But the wily cat wiggles free and zips under the sofa, and I do a world record belly flop right onto the hardwood floors. Note to self: take your mother up on the offer to gift you one of her antique oriental rugs.

"Lemon? Everything okay in there?" I recognize that surly tone. It's Everett.

"Just peachy!"

"What was that thump?" he growls as if my acrobatics offended him on some level.

"An experiment in how many ribs I can crack from couch diving. If it's an Olympic sport, I think I have a shot at medaling."

The door swings open and in rushes a frozen hurricane-like wind.

"Dear Lord, close that," I snip as Dutch the demon dog bounds happily from one end of the room to the other. In his defense, he simply looks like he's having a great time. Who knows how long it's been since he's stretched those beautiful legs? His long, glossy mane glows ethereal in the light, and he really is a gorgeous specimen. He calms down long enough to walk in a circle before coming over and attempting to lick my forehead. "You are such a love! What a handsome, sweet boy—yes, you are," I say, struggling to get on all fours myself, and Everett helps hoist me up the rest of the way.

"Thank you." He takes a half-step back. "I think."

"Not you." I wave him off before reaching under the couch and extricating my poor sweet cat. "I was talking to the dog. Which, by the way, is why Pancake is completely out of sorts."

Dutch whimpers before lying down and covering his eyes with his paws.

"The dog?" Everett gives a curious look around without moving a muscle in his body. Even though Everett is trying his best to understand my peculiar supernatural capabilities, I can tell the struggle to submit to his black and white view of life demands to win over. His eyes widen as he looks to me. "*That dog?*"

"Yes, *that* dog," I say, plopping down on the sofa with Pancake, and up bounds the exuberant retriever and plops himself right next to us. Pancake's nails dig right through my velvet emerald dress and sink into my skin. "Ouch," I yelp before ribbing the pooch. "Would you mind scooting over? You really are crowding me."

"Lemon, you're scaring me. What is that dog doing here? And if I'm not mistaken, your cat isn't too thrilled with the idea."

"You're perceptive. To answer your questions, I don't know—and you are correct. Pancake seems to be picking up on him just like he picked up on your father the day we moved into the neighborhood." Everett moved in next door the same day I took up occupancy here. His father sort of christened the place as far as any spooktacular presence goes. "His name is Dutch, and I'm guessing he belonged to Tanner, but I have no clue why I can't seem to shake him. He seems to have a superior intelligence." The pretty pooch lifts his head, and his lips curve to the ceiling as if accepting the adulation. "And he's absolutely adorable—if not for those glowing ruby eyes of fire. It's a bit off-putting." Dutch whimpers, and I give him a quick scratch between the ears, and oddly enough, Pancake begins to purr. "Finally. I think they've both settled down. Now to you, Judge Baxter. Why in the heck did you leave my sister out of your sight? She's a lead suspect in Tanner's murder—as is Forest."

"As are you."

"No way. Nobody believes I did it."

He inches back. That crimped scowl lets me know he's amused. "Why would they? You screamed at him not once but twice tonight, and you were found with the murder weapon in your hand—while hovering over his motionless body."

I shrink a little in my seat. "Yes, well, you see— Oh good Lord, you're right. Soon enough, they'll accuse me of being the package thief, too. But I swear I'm innocent, Your Honor. I swear on Tanner Redwood's Golden Retriever I didn't do it."

"Lemon, you don't need to plead your case with me. You already did that, remember? And I happened to side with you on that matter as I side with you on this."

"We caught him with two different women in the span of an hour. Do you think it was one of them?"

"I don't know. All I know about the guy is that he looked like someone I'd have locked up on Christmas Eve."

"Lainey should have thrown the book at him months ago. And really, Everett? You let my sweet, innocent sister, the librarian, give you the slip?"

"She's wily—much like her sister. Besides, she said she had to use the ladies' room. I wasn't going to follow her in there. So I waited."

"Why do I sense a but coming on?"

He takes a moment to glower at me. "*But*—before she could come out, I heard a horrible crash outside, and as luck would have it, I saw a pair of taillights speeding away."

I suck in a breath and swat him with a throw pillow. "You must have seen the murderer in their getaway car! What make? What model? Wait—are those the same thing? Never mind all that. What color was it?"

"I didn't see anything other than the red glow of lights, but I'm willing to guess the car was either silver or white."

"How do you know?"

He pulls out his phone and holds it between us as a picture pops up on the screen. "I went outside and found some broken glass under this minivan. The van is black or navy blue, I couldn't tell, but see those lines?"

"Yes," I say, pulling the phone forward and inspecting three clean white striations.

"I figure the car that struck the van was a pale color."

"Wow, that's a nasty little dent they left as a parting gift. Did you tell Noah?"

"That's the thing. I went back into the foyer of the community center to check on your sister, and by the time I figured out she was no longer in there, the minivan was gone, too. I tried to tell Noah, but he blew me off." His lips flicker in annoyance. "However, I think I've just told a far more experienced detective." He leans in and brushes his finger over my nose. "What about you? I bet you already have this figured out."

"Nope. In fact, my sister and Forest were both pretty hostile this evening. It wouldn't surprise me at all if Forest ditched the sheriff. He might be twenty minutes into Canada by now trying to outrun homicide charges. Forest hated Tanner."

"What kind of car does Forest drive?"

My eyes expand the size of snowballs. "A silver Mustang."

"I guess we know who Noah will be paying a visit to come morning."

"No way. Noah cannot find out. I'm positive Forest didn't do this. I'll handle this one on my own." My heart thumps wildly in my chest. "There's just no way that Forest killed Tanner."

Everett's chest thunders with a dull laugh. "You're not going alone. I get off work at two. December is a light month."

"Fine. But I'm only letting you come along because I like your company. I'm perfectly capable of delivering cookies to the firehouse all on my own." My nose twitches the way it does when I'm fighting a good cry. "Every time I go back to that firehouse, I swear I can feel my daddy there."

He rattles my knee with his hand. "It doesn't always get easier, does it? That's another reason for me to be there with you. I can commiserate. Ever since my dad and I made up, I miss him on a whole new level."

"I'm so glad you had a chance to make amends."

He nods as his eyes magnetize over mine, and I'd swear there were tears glistening in them. He takes in a sharp breath. "So, I guess Noah will be popping by soon. It's prom night, right?" His brows bounce, and a bite of embarrassment rips through me.

"It was going to be. But he's a little tied up. We've decided to reschedule."

"Reschedule?" He shakes his head wistfully as he heads to the entry. "That sounds like a Noah move." He turns my way as he's about to duck out the door. His lids hood low, and a hint of dirty intention twitches at his lips. "Just for the record, Lemon, I don't pencil in the important things. I let them happen as often and as loud as they want."

An audible gulp escapes me.

"Night."

He leaves with a click of the door, and both Dutch and Pancake give a forlorn look in that direction as if they were sorry he was gone.

"I sort of wish he hung around, too," I whisper.

There's been another murder in Honey Hollow, and not only did they take Tanner's life, they erased my good time with Noah.

And as shallow as it sounds, I'm equally ticked about both.

CHAPTER 5

⁂

The Naughty Hottie Book Club is a bawdy compilation of both Naomi Turner's rather new literary endeavor and my mother's historical fiction book club defects. There's really just a handful of my mother's cohorts who wanted in on the younger set's sexy reads. This month's salacious selection is *Santa's Ho Ho Hos*, a steamy read about the horny head elf himself and a bevy of naughty North Pole beauties. It sounds perfectly perverted, and I'm thrilled I was too busy with the bakery to partake in the madness.

The Cutie Pie Bakery and Cakery is the scene of this literary crime. It's where Naomi—Keelie's twin, but you wouldn't know it with those long, dark locks, her sour disposition—Lily Swanson, along with my sister, and just about every woman in Honey Hollow sit at the edge of their seat giggling and gasping as Naomi reads a steamy excerpt out loud. The entire left side of the bakery gets up en mass and heads for the exit as Naomi acts out every gasp and moan.

"Would you keep it G-rated?" I hiss as I refill their coffees with a painted-on smile. "Or I'll have to rethink hosting this sexual scholastic endeavor."

Keelie waves me off. "If she gives us the boot, we'll hightail it to the Honey Pot next door. There's no way we're letting Ms. Prissy Pants put a damper on our good time. She's just steaming mad because that murder last night put the kibosh on the penciled in nookie she was supposed to have with that detective boyfriend of hers."

"*Keelie!*" And what is with the penciling in analogy? First Everett and now Keelie. My mind wanders to that double heart I drew onto my calendar last week. It might be true, but still.

My mother gasps with delight, as do Eve Hollister and Chrissy Nash. Eve is the co-leader of the OG book club, and Chrissy Nash is the mayor's ex-wife. Mayor Nash was cheating on her with about a dozen different women, and he hasn't let up yet. Sadly, it sounds as if Tanner and the mayor had a lot in common.

Hey? Maybe whoever offed Tanner is a serial killer bent on eliminating the cheats of the world and they've decided to start in Honey Hollow? If that's the case, then Mayor Nash had better watch his back. And maybe they steal packages because they're too busy to shop what with all the killing to be had. Makes total sense.

"Aw"—my mother grabs ahold of my left hand—"my little lady is on her way to becoming a woman. I'd hold out for the ring if I were you."

Eve, the woman who looks as if she could be my mother's *mother* but is shockingly the same age, shakes her head. "Never you mind the ring, honey. The clock is ticking. I say go for the baby. At the end of the day, the ring may not stick around for as long as you'd like. But kids—they're the gift that keep on giving."

"Hear, hear." Chrissy lifts her mug as if she were toasting. "Have some fun while the fun is ripe for the picking." She lowers her cup to the table with a thunk. It's only then I notice that her eyes are red and glossy, her face puffy as if she's been crying. I bet Mayor Nash was flashing some pretty young thing in front of poor Chrissy last night. Sadly, it's not a shocker. He can be a cad like that.

Eve wraps an arm around her. "Oh, hon. It will get easier in time. Why don't you get yourself one of those young bucks? You know, the ones who'll shag whatever moves? You'd be surprised what a delicious night of sin can do for you."

Mom chortles as if she too were apprised. "The medicinal benefits alone are well worth it. Do you realize you need to stimulate those hormones or they'll just dry up and disappear? Dry *up!*"

"My word up in heaven," I moan as I top off their coffee in a fury. The last thing I want to hear is a dissertation on the benefits of sex espoused by my mother.

Chrissy wads up a napkin and dabs her eyes. "I've got to run." She no sooner hitches her purse over her shoulder than she's out the door.

Eve cups a hand around her mouth. "I agree, honey. There's no time like the present!"

She and Mom chortle up another storm before they exchange high fives.

"Mother, I don't think she was scampering off to find the nearest young buck. I think she was really upset."

She averts her eyes at the thought. "She's just really upset that we're right. But don't you worry about Chrissy." Her shoulders do that salacious wiggle that makes me squirm. "She's hinted at the fact she has a paramour. And he's a young buck indeed."

"Who? Who?" Eve does a poor impersonation of an owl.

Mom shakes her head. "She wouldn't say. But he's the reason she's had pep in her step as of late. I hope she brings him to the tree lighting to really give Mayor Nash a taste of his own medicine."

"That will be the day." I make my way to the other end of the lewd literary society just as Lily is finishing up a salacious tale of her own.

"And when I woke up, I tiptoed on out. I like to keep my morning look a mystery for as long as I can."

"What's this?" Something in me stirs to life at the thought of Lily ditching Everett for someone more her trashy speed. "Who's the unlucky fella?" I give a sly wink. Lily and I aren't nearly as hostile as we used to be before she worked at the Cutie Pie. Dare I say, we might even be friends now.

"Essex," she hisses his name like a dirty secret, and I gasp as if I just inhaled an entire handful of chocolate chips.

"Es who?" The carafe nearly slips out of my hand.

Lily rolls her eyes. "Everett, to you. I've graduated to calling him by his real name." Her shoulders bounce in turn as if every last inch of her approved of this news.

"Oh my word, you spent the night with Everett?" I can't get my head around this.

He spent the night with Lily of all people? She's practically my worst enemy in the world. How could he do this to me?

"That's right." Her eyes sparkle as if someone lit a match and stuck it in her ear. "And look at this." She fishes a pair of odd-shaped silver earrings out of her pocket. "They're cufflinks, Lottie. And they're his. Everyone knows that cufflinks are the new class ring." She takes off with a smirk riding on her smug face.

I suck in a sharp breath just as Dutch barks and bounds his way over. The adorable phantasm hopped right into the van with me this morning and made a sport of chasing his tail around the kitchen island. He's quite the entertaining cutie—at least to me since I am the only one capable of witnessing his glory. It's a shame, though. A beast as regal as he is should be appreciated by all. Well—maybe with the exception of those glowing red eyes. I don't think anyone would appreciate those much. I'd ask him to tone down the supernatural if I thought he could do it.

Keelie hops up next to me. "I have to get back to the grind, but I just have to say I really am sorry things didn't work out for you. How about you roll with the punches and let him find a little Lottie treat snuggling under his covers tonight? Slip into that naughty nightie I bought you, and once he flicks on those bedroom lights, he'll find the gift of a lifetime. *You*."

"Keelie, if I hide out in his bed, he's liable to pull a gun on me. Breaking and entering in a detective's house is not the brightest idea. Unless, of course, your plan is to put an end to me."

"My plan is to end your dry spell." She gifts me a peck on the cheek and takes off for the Honey Pot.

The Honey Pot is conjoined with the Cutie Pie Bakery through an entry that was made in our shared wall. It was my ex's, Bear's, doing. He did the renovation and made sure to have it all done in record time. In fact, the large resin oak tree that sits planted in the middle of the Honey Pot and its twinkle light strung branches that graze over the ceiling were graciously extended through the café portion of the Cutie Pie. It was a gift from Nell and Keelie, but it was Bear's handiwork that helped pull it off.

Lainey comes up, looking forlorn.

"I'm surprised to see you here. You should have taken the day off," I whisper as I pull her into a firm embrace.

"I did, but I couldn't stare at the walls another minute. I needed to get out." She makes a face. "I came by to get coffee and got an earful of things I want to know nothing about. Did you hear that thing with the sleigh bells? Do people really do that?"

"It's fiction, Lainey. *Dangerous* fiction. The human body isn't made to do ninety percent of those freaky things."

Mom crops up. "All right, you two. Sorry to break up the party, but I need to take off. Lottie, can I order three-dozen Christmas tree crunchies for the B&B? Oh, and about a dozen or so Bones of the Dead? I like to keep it festive this time of year."

Lainey gags on cue.

"Oh, you." Mother brushes her off. "They're traditional Italian Christmas cookies, and I happen to have an entire enclave of Italian tourists staying with me."

"You bet," I say. "I can have them to you later today."

"Perfect. I'm having dinner with Bradley tonight." Her entire body gyrates when she says it.

"Mother! I'm warning you. Stay far, far away from him. He's nothing but trouble. The two women he was with are dead and in prison respectively. Lord only knows where you'll end up."

A rumbling laugh brews deep within her. "I already know. It's the *bedroom*," she whispers that last word out, and yet it's still far too loud. "Ta-ta!" She takes off with a wave of her fingers.

Lainey moans as she makes her way to the door. "I'm going to throw up now."

"Oh, hey"— I trot over—"what happened with you and Forest last night?"

She bites down on her lip. The guilt on her face is thick enough to frost a cake. "He stayed most of the night. He's working today, but he said he'd swing by again tonight. I said I'd pick up a pizza in case he was hungry."

"Oh, he'll be hungry. It just won't be for pizza." I wince at the inappropriate timing of it all. "Any news from Tanner's family?"

"His sister Rachel thinks I'm the devil. His mother says she'll keep me posted as far as arrangements go. Oh, and hey, remember his brother Hook? He's coming back for the funeral."

"No kidding?" Hook Redwood was quite the looker back in high school. He was a year older than me. Graduated valedictorian. "Did you know he went to Yale?"

"Did you know he's a stock broker in New York?"

I can't help but make a face at the mention of the city. After I caught Bear with one too many women trapped in his paws— none of which were me—I took off for Columbia University with no intention of ever coming back. Long story short, I met yet another boy who also had a penchant for women who were not me, so I hightailed it back to Honey Hollow.

"Well, good for Hook. I look forward to seeing him at the funeral."

"You're going to Tanner's funeral? You could hardly stand the guy—and you were caught with the murder weapon in your hand."

"Yes, well, I seem to like some people a whole lot better once they're dead. Besides, historically speaking, the guilty party usually bothers to show up to see their work completed, if you know what I mean."

She sucks in a breath. "Geez, I hope not. Can you imagine? A murderer in our midst. And at Christmas!"

"Go get your pizza. Let me worry about murderers and Christmas." Two words I never thought I'd say in a sentence.

Lainey takes off just as Everett walks in with his dark inky suit, that perma scowl on his face.

"Lemon."

"Essex?" I catch him off guard a moment. "Oh, wait, I haven't graduated to proper names. *Lily* has." Now it's me scowling at him.

His chin ticks up a notch. "I may have had a visitor last night."

"Did you know that visitor lifted your cufflinks? She thinks they're the new class ring." I resist the urge to swat him.

Everett frowns at the thought and holds up his bare sleeve. "They were my only pair, and you're right. They were lifted indeed."

Dutch comes over and touches his paw to my hip.

"Hey, you," I whisper, giving him a quick scratch behind the ears. "It looks as if we both had a visitor last night who was missing a few brain cells." I lean toward the ruby-eyed pooch. "When it comes to you, I'm only being literal. You're smart as a whip and so very handsome—yes, you are."

"Lottie?" a male voice booms next to me, and I look up to find Noah Corbin Fox looking both vexingly sexy and shockingly confused. "Who are you talking to?"

"Oh!" I glance to Everett, who looks as if he's resisting the urge to laugh. "Essex—um, Everett—I mean, Judge Baxter." I straighten with the lie. "He was telling me that he had a lady caller spend the night, and I was simply doing an impersonation of how I thought things went." I give a little shrug, uncertain myself if I'm buying the bull I've just heaped all over the Cutie Pie.

"Ah." Noah looks to his former stepbrother. "What are you doing here?" His voice drops an octave, and any trace of humanity dissipates as he glowers his way.

"I volunteered to help Lottie bring cookies to the firehouse."

"The firehouse." Noah nods my way, amused. "Why do I get the feeling you're interfering in yet another one of my investigations?" Noah is not crazy about the fact I've injected myself into his investigations before. And, apparently, Everett has no problem outing me.

"Nope. Not me." I do a poor job of crossing my heart, and instead look as if I were trying to distract him by way of the girls. "It's just a thing I do at Christmas. Everett asked if he could tag along and see the exact spot Joseph Lemon discovered me all those years ago." It's true. My adoptive father found me at the firehouse and brought me home to Mama, and the rest is Lemon family history.

"I see." Noah inches back, inspecting me. "Well, it just so happens that I was headed there next myself. Mind if I tag along?"

"Not at all. Let me grab the cookies."

I'll distract Noah with more than just my cookies, and that should give Everett enough time to inspect Forest's Mustang.

Ready or not, Noah Corbin Fox. I'm coming for your investigation.

CHAPTER 6

*oney Hollow shines in a special way during each of the four seasons, but Christmastime in our cozy little town is truly a wonder. A fresh blanket of snow smooths the landscape like a fresh layer of heavenly icing. The scent of the evergreens fills the air, and there's a bit of Christmas magic everywhere you look.

I hitch a ride to the firehouse with Noah, and we meet up with Everett in the parking lot. An entire line of cars sits parked alongside the firehouse, and the lot extends toward the back of the building where I'm guessing Forest's Mustang happens to be since there's not a silver car in sight. The skies are dark, and

45

another storm is threatening to dust our world with powder later tonight.

Dutch barks up a riot as we get out of the car. That's right. Dutch. This fiercely loyal Golden Retriever is living up to his calling, long after the living is through.

I can't say I mind too much. Growing up, we never had big dogs, and I always wanted one just like this with long, luscious locks. He's so stately and handsome, I'm starting to feel as if I've got a big protector around me at all times.

Although, I still don't have a clue why he's with me. Does it mean something? Does he simply like the way I smell? Does he have a mad hankering for a batch of fresh baked doggie treats? Honestly, the possibilities are endless, and I have zero ideas on how to solve this puzzle.

"Whatcha got there?" Noah asks as I carefully peel the foil off the platter.

"Just a few chocolate chip blondies, eggnog truffles, cinnamon shortbread, stained glass windows, peppermint pinwheels, chocolate crinkle cookies, and my signature gingerbread boys and girls." I hand him a gingerbread girl, and he gives a naughty moan as he bites into her.

Noah's lids are hooded low, and that goofy grin on his face lets me know he's just as interested in the baker as he is the cookie.

"What's going on?" Everett gives his lapel a quick tug, so I give him a gingerbread girl as well. "Why thank you, Lemon. This is exactly how I take my women, spontaneously and as the moment arises." A dirty chuckle strums from his throat as he gives Noah the stink eye.

"What's that look for?" Noah squints as if he was reading him. "I know that look. That was a dig at me, wasn't it?" His head tips to the side, and you can practically see the cogs turning in his brain. "Wait a minute." Noah inches back. His eyes cut to mine, laced with suspicion. "Lottie," he says rife with disappointment. "You didn't tell Everett, did you?"

"She told me," Everett the rat mumbles through a bite. "I'm pretty sure she told Keelie." He nudges my arm with his elbow. "Did you show him the nightie?"

"Would you shush!"

"What nightie?" Noah's eyes have reduced to slits, his shoulders are squared over his chest, and he looks rough and tough and every bit delicious.

"There's no nightie." I shake my head just so at the ornery judge who apparently left his muzzle back at the courthouse.

"There's a nightie." Everett's lips curve with the hint of a malevolent smile. "It was red and see-through and had this frilly white fluff. I believe it was designed to curl Mr. Claus' toes." He looks to Noah. "And that, my red-faced friend, would be you."

A nervous giggle escapes me. Noah is rather red-faced, but it has less to do with embarrassment and more to do with rage. But, nonetheless, the nightie was left at the community center, and I have no intention on going back to the scene of the crime to excavate it.

A woman's high-pitched cackle emits from behind, and we see none other than Ivy Fairbanks strutting out of the firehouse along with Scooter McPhee, the chief. Scooter actually worked with my father. He's quite a bit younger than my father was, his pepper black hair has yet to see any salt, and he's built like a building, ready and willing to risk his life in any situation as are all of the men and women who work here.

"Lottie!" Chief McPhee lifts a friendly hand. "There's something I've been meaning to give you. Let me see if I can track it down. I'll be right back." He takes off as Ivy strides over in her far too cute black leather boots that come up high over her knees.

She's wearing a winter white wool coat that hangs open in the front paired with black jeans and a simple black sweater, and I can't but think she really did step out of a magazine. I don't ever look that put together. On my best day you won't find a dusting of flour on my face or clothes, but that's few and far between.

It would figure she's here.

"What are we laughing at?" She lifts her nose to Everett as if she understood he was her only hope of ratting us out. And, well, he most likely is.

"Lemon and Noah are contemplating knocking boots."

My mouth falls open, but before I can reprimand him, Ivy pipes up.

"Ah yes. The canceled coitus." She folds her arms across her chest while inspecting us with a smug look of satisfaction. I'd ask Dutch to sic her, but the only thing he's capable of doing is licking her to death. And, believe you me, if death was truly involved, I'd give him the go-ahead.

I swat Noah and risk dropping all my cookies in the snow. "You told her?"

"You told him." He nods to Everett.

"And I deeply regret it," I growl at the judge and mean it.

Everett snatches another gingerbread girl off the platter—it would so figure. "Don't forget the best friend and the nightie. Trust me, buddy, you need to see the nightie."

Ivy sniffs the air between us. "Detective Fox, I've got a new lead. I'll see you at the office." Her persimmon-colored lips expand in my direction, and not in any kind way. "Sorry if this impedes on your carnal calendar, but he'll be mine for the rest of the evening." She looks to him. "I'll pick up a pizza from Mangia on my way back to the station."

I suck in a lungful of frozen Honey Hollow air as she takes off in her government-issued ride. "Carnal calendar? And pizza from Mangia? That's *our* thing." It comes out a little louder than I meant for it to. Oh heck, I meant for it.

Noah cringes. "She asked what my favorite pizza place was

the other night. Sorry." He practically mouths the word. "How about we get those cookies inside?"

The three of us head in, with one of us a heck of a lot less cheery than I was five minutes ago. Soon, an entire herd of men dressed in yellow swarm us, and by the time I put the platter down onto the table, it's empty.

Forest smiles that warm smile I miss so very much. He's so shockingly handsome, it almost makes me want to sock my sister the next time I see her. How could she have wasted all those precious months with a bonehead like Tanner when a perfectly good heartthrob like Forest was let off the leash? Although, now that he's gone, I feel terrible for referring to him as a bonehead.

"Lottie, you outdid yourself. Those were delicious."

"Well, thank you. Next time I know to bring three times the amount."

We share a warm laugh before Forest and Chief McPhee give us a quick tour of the garage. The firehouse was gifted a brand new truck recently, and he spends some time showing off all of its technological bells and whistles.

He looks to me, and a general sadness sweeps over him. That's usually a cue people are about to bring up my father. Joseph Lemon was such a sweet and gentle man that to this very day he's still sincerely missed by many.

"Sorry. It took a second for me to dig it out. I left it back in the dining hall."

"No problem. We'll come with you." I glare over at Everett, and he lifts a brow.

"Right." Everett nods my way. "I've got a quick call to make. I'll be out front."

Perfect. This should be plenty of time to distract Noah while Everett looks for a dented Mustang—or hopefully, a lack thereof.

Forest pulls Noah and me to the side as the chief heads over to the desk in the corner.

"Lottie, what the hell happened last night? Did you get the killer?"

Noah's chest expands the size of the door. "The investigation is well underway, and we are combing through hundreds of viable leads."

"Hundreds?" Quite frankly, I'm wondering if he added one too many zeros to his estimate.

"Yes, hundreds." Noah warms my back with his hand. "I promise you, this investigation will wrap up quickly."

Truthfully, I'm caught off guard that Noah seems so confident. I bet Ivy was here, because she already knew about the potential dent in Forest's car. But a small part of me finds it difficult to believe. Not that I don't think Noah is capable. I'm positive Noah is far more than capable. In fact, I bet he has capable hands, too. And if it wasn't for Ivy and that pizza from Mangia she was trying to lure him away with, I'd have those capable hands on me in just a few hours.

"Well, I didn't do it." Forest sets his feet in a defiant stance as he tries to clear his name. "I know what it looked like. I yelled at the guy. I threatened him."

"You took off in his wake," I remind him.

"Gee, thanks, Lot."

"Not to worry," Noah says to Forest. "The investigation still has her pinned as the number one suspect." He ticks his head my way, and I gasp.

"Forest?" I look up at him in a desperate attempt to clear my name. "What did you see when you ran out that back corridor? Did you see anyone at all? Suspicious vehicles?"

"Not a thing. In fact, I marveled that the guy disappeared into thin air." He steps in close. "One of my buddies here filled me in on some pretty unsavory things about good old Redwood." He glowers when he says his name. His disdain for the guy is still pretty palpable. "That guy had a revolving door of women. How could Lainey have wanted him anywhere near her? She's sweet and kind, and not in any way like the girls Tanner is used to."

Noah's shoulders bounce. "Maybe he liked the change of pace?"

"Well, I'm sorry he's dead, but I'm glad it's over." Forest blinks over at me. "Hook is in town. He'll be here for the funeral. I never did understand how the same family could produce such vastly different offspring. Their sister Rachel seems to have her head screwed on straight, and Hook is the real deal—but Tanner, apart from work, he couldn't get his fill of women."

The chief comes back, and Forest takes off with a nod.

"This was your father's." He holds out a thick silver ring with an impression of the company's emblem. "It slipped behind his desk. Found it when we were doing some renovating."

"Oh my goodness! It's so precious." I touch it to my chest and close my eyes. I can see him there in my mind's eye. His gentle blue eyes, the way his entire face lit up when any of us Lemon women stepped into the room. My father was a true gentleman, a man's man, a sweet soul who deserved to live far longer than fate determined. "Thank you so much." I blink back tears from my eyes. "It's as if he's delivering one last Christmas gift to my mother. I'll be sure to wrap it up for her. This is truly special."

We say goodbye to the chief and meet with Everett just as we're about to leave.

"How did the phone call go?" My heart thumps wildly with fear. Forest all but shouted that he didn't do it, and now I'm wondering if he did protest too much.

"Not a scratch on the fender. Everything worked out fine."

Noah leers at him. "What kind of a euphemism is that?"

"One only the elite understand." His chest bucks with a silent laugh. "It's something I made up *spontaneously*. I realize that's another three-dollar word for you, but it might behoove you to look that one up." He shoots him with his finger. "The nightie will be worth it, believe me."

Noah growls at his old stepbrother just as Everett hops into his fancy ride and takes off.

We head out, and Noah wraps his arms around me before I can climb into his truck. "You and Everett wouldn't have happened to be looking for something on say—somebody's fender, were you?"

My mouth opens and I'm about to tell him everything, especially now that Forest is in the clear, but then I remember that he and Ivy have already amassed hundreds of clues. I'd hate to give them something else to keep them with pizza at three in the morning.

"Nope. Not a thing."

"Good." His dimples dig in deep, his lids grow heavy and thick, a dangerous combination that makes all of my girl parts beg to combust. "Now about that nightie…"

"You won't get a clue from me. You'll simply have to make time to see me in it." I cringe a little because it just so happens it was left in the melee at the community center. But I'm sure Keelie will be more than glad to help me hunt down a replacement.

"Is there any way to bribe you into bringing along some cookies?" That playful tone of his makes me insane to pull him into the nearest snow bank and have my way with him.

"Just cookies? I'll bring some frosting along to make things interesting."

"Oh, sweetie"—his voice dips low—"I will certainly frost your cookies."

My stomach bisects with heat, and I give a soft moan.

"In that case, one of us had better find Tanner Redwood's killer, and soon. I believe you promised me three days of heaven."

"It's a darn good start, and we will certainly be touching paradise."

Noah's dirty grin doesn't even have time to crest before he lands those lips to mine and gives me a taste of eternally blissful things to come.

As terrible as it sounds, even in death, Tanner Redwood has found a way to infuriate me.

Well-played, Tanner. Well-played.

CHAPTER 7

The Cutie Pie Bakery and Cakery has never seen so much foot traffic, and if this keeps up, we might just need new flooring by the new year. They're beginning to wear a path to the register—never a bad thing. Honestly, Keelie has lent me five more staff members from the Honey Pot. Ironically, the Honey Pot's foot traffic has decreased slightly. It turns out, with all the office parties, school parties, ugly sweater parties, tree trimming parties, and parties just to have parties, people are far more eager to pick up a box of cookies and a Yule log beforehand rather than stopping in for a nice hot meal.

By the time the bakery closes, I'm well past exhausted. But

despite my aching dogs, the ones attached to my feet, my newfound dog, Dutch, and I pile into the van and head out to the Jolly Holly Tree Lot where Everett is waiting for me.

It looks as if my newfound angel of a pet with the glowing eyes is sticking around for the long haul, or at least until he figures out how to eat those cookies he drools after all day long. Pancake hasn't exactly made peace with him yet, although in Pancake's defense, I'm not sure he knows what it is. All he seems to realize is that there's a disturbance in the force, and it's trying to eat his dinner.

If, and when, we catch Tanner's killer, it will be interesting to see what happens to my new furry friend. I admit I'm getting used to having him around. He's ventured into places in the bakery I wouldn't dream of letting Pancake tunnel into. And it makes me feel better when I talk to him on the drive to and from work. I don't feel like such a loon carrying on these conversations on my own. In my defense, talking to yourself is a great way to process your day—especially if you're detangling a murder investigation.

"You're going to love the tree lot. Tons of open space for you to bounce around in. I sort of wish I'd brought a Frisbee along. Although, I'm not really a fan of running in the snow."

Dutch sighs as if he wishes I were.

Once we arrive, I spot Everett right away. Dutch leaps out of the car without the use of the door and begins barking and jumping as if he's never been outside before. He darts into the woods while I head for my favorite legal eagle. Mr. Sexy is indeed living up to that mouthwatering moniker the baristas of the world have gifted him.

"Judge Baxter. You look dapper per usual."

"Evening, Lemon. Do you have a tree?"

"Not yet. Noah and I were—"

"About to pencil it in?" A dark chuckle comes from him.

"Noah might be all about planning, but I'm all about action. I think we're getting you a tree."

"I can't get a tree without Noah. You get a tree."

"I have a tree. I keep it in a box in the attic."

"Very funny."

"I don't value a sense of humor. Besides, you and I both know we're not here for a tree, and yet without one we're sure to arouse suspicion."

"You're so right!" I sling an arm around him and pull him into a partial hug. "You're always thinking on your feet."

Lainey let me know that Tanner Redwood's second in command—now the head of the Parks and Recs Department by proxy—is a man by the name of Pete Winslow. Pete happens to moonlight at the tree lot, and I couldn't pass up a chance to speak with him.

We spot him over by the register, tall and lanky with large glowing gray eyes just the way Lainey described, and the fact he has a miniature stocking attached to his chest with the name *PETE* scrawled over it just tipped my assurance over the edge.

"Can I help you?" He has a friendly demeanor about him, and there's just something that makes you instantly like the guy. Pretty much the opposite of Tanner.

"Looking for a tree," Everett responds just as chipper, and I have to admire what a good actor he can be when needed. Lord knows there isn't a chipper bone in Everett's body.

"Great." Pete dives into his spiel, orienting us as to where the nobles and firs are and how much it is per foot. "We've been seeing a lot of nice couples just like you folks tonight. I don't care what anyone says. This is the most romantic time of the year."

It's only then I realize I still have my arm frozen around Everett's waist. In my defense, he is very warm. Have I mentioned the snow?

A low, seductive laugh belts from Everett's chest. "She just can't keep her hands off of me. Isn't that right, Cupcake?"

"*Cupcake?*" I blink up at him, unsure of how I feel about this newly minted moniker. On one hand, it's a very endearing nod to my profession. But on the other hand, it's a classic putdown of the female species. "Yes, Sugar Puss. Sometimes it's just impossible to get enough of you." Like when I'm in the mood to kill, or maim. I glance back to Pete. "Hey, rumor has it, you've lost one of your own. I'm really sorry to hear it."

Everett grunts as if disapproving of my segue. I'll admit, the transition wasn't smooth, but it works in a pinch. Exactly how long does he want me to hold onto his waist anyhow?

Pete grimaces. "We lost Tanner Redwood. It was brutal. I heard there was some psychopath hovering over him with an icicle in her hand."

"Excuse me? *Psychopath?*"

Everett wraps his arm around my own waist and gives a slight squeeze as if keeping me in check before leaning in. "Sounds like love gone sour to me."

Okay, so Everett's approach borders on brilliant, but it doesn't change the fact I'm irate that my sanity has been called into question. Hover over one dead body and you're in need of a straitjacket.

"I can see that happening." Pete gives a wistful shake of the head. "That dude had more women crawling over him than ants on a dirt mound covered with honey."

Everett bounces with agreement. "That will do it. So, which one do you think did it? I'm sure he brought a few around."

"I don't know. The librarian was the quiet one. But they say it's usually the quiet ones you need to look out for."

"Wait a minute—" An incredulous laugh belts from me. Call me psycho, fine, but paint my big sis as a killer and you'll have another—

Everett clears his throat. "You're right. But what about the wild ones? You know that old saying, *when you hear hoofbeats in Central Park, you don't go looking for zebras.*"

"You got me there." He scratches the back of his neck. "There's Bella. I can't say he's brought her around, but she sure made several unannounced appearances, if you know what I mean. Those were closed-door visits when she popped in. Sometimes, they went on for hours at a time." He lifts a brow to Everett as if sharing a machismo moment in honor of Tanner's insatiable libido.

"Bella Lipmann?" I say her name with glee as if we were old friends. And I'm sure we would be—if she existed.

"Bella"—he snaps his fingers as he squints toward the sky— "Carter!" He points a finger my way. "That's it. Young, redhead."

"Oh, right! Bella Carter. I just saw her. My goodness where did I see her?" Playing hide-and-seek with something in Santa's pants, but that's another story. "Oh, she works at that place"—I snap my fingers at him as if I had a clue.

Pete lifts a hand as if he understands why I might be remiss to say it out loud. "Bazingas."

"Bazingas?" Everett and I say in unison. It's sort of nice to hear our voices harmonize that way.

"You know"—Pete looks around before leaning in and cupping his hands over his chest—"*Bazingas.*"

Everett chuckles. "It's a restaurant in Leeds, Lemon. Need I say more?"

"No," I flatline as the picture comes in clear. I'm guessing Everett will volunteer for Bazingas duty before the night is through. "How about that brunette? The one with short hair, cute face?" I've got enough on Bella. Moving on.

Pete's face lights up. "Kelly Ferdinand. Yeah, geez. That's another nutcase. She used to work for Parks and Rec in Ashford. That's how we met her. Known her for years. She finally finished with her schooling." He averts his eyes a moment. "If you could call it schooling considering her profession."

"Oh, I know!" I say, suddenly realizing I have no clue where to go next. But it's served me well before.

Everett warms my arm. "What's Kelly up to these days?"

"I'm not saying it." I give a coy laugh as if willing to guard her secret to the grave.

Pete lifts his hands. "Hey, me either." He backs away. "Let me know if you need anything else."

Shoot. Think quickly!

"We sure will!" I shout as if we're about to take off. "Oh, wait, let's not be sexist. Surely there was a guy in the mix that could have been angry enough to off the poor man." Yes! It's hard to go wrong when you're playing the gender card. It's one female against two males. I win hands down.

"That's easy"—Pete takes a few steps toward us once again—"there's only one dude who couldn't stand the guy. Tim Wagner. He still thinks Tanner was the one who got him fired."

"Was he?" It begged the question, so I had to ask.

"I guess we'll never know."

He takes off, and I quickly pull out my phone and take notes. *Bella Carter, Bazingas, Kelly Ferdinand, big question mark, and Tim Wagner, fired and angry about it.*

"All right, Lemon"—Everett nods toward the trees staring us down—"let's pick out a good one. It's on me."

I take Everett up on his offer, and we end up hauling a seven-foot shaggy Douglas fir into my living room.

Still no sign of Noah's truck across the street, and it makes my stomach sour to think about all the pizza he's enjoying with Poison Ivy. I hope she's lactose intolerant by Christmas. A gift from the universe to me. After all those corpses it's sent me, I think I deserve it.

Everett helps me set the bushy tree on its base, and he even twines a string of twinkle lights on it while Pancake and I watch in wonder.

"There you go," he says, returning to an upright position. "Holiday magic."

"Thanks, Everett. This means a lot to me."

"My pleasure." He gives Pancake a quick pat over the head. "Is that all he does is hang out on the arm of your sofa all day?"

"Is there anything better?"

"Does he have his own bed? Because that might be better. Poor guy looks as if he's about to roll right off."

"He doesn't need a bed. He sleeps with me."

"At least there's one male on the planet that can say that and it isn't Noah Fox." A quick rubber band grin rides on his lips.

"I'm about to throw a pillow at you."

"Hold your fire," he says as he heads for the exit. "And, Lemon? See you at Bazingas tomorrow night for dinner."

Knew it.

No sooner does the door close than a scratching sound emits from the other side. I head over and open it to find the cutest overgrown Golden Retriever—albeit a somewhat haunted version panting up a storm.

"There you are," I say, letting him in. "I wondered if I'd ever see you again."

And yet, a part of me was certain.

I curl up on the couch with Dutch and Pancake on either side of me while I Google Kelly Ferdinand, but there's nothing. Huh. I look up Bella and the keyword *Bazingas* and, sure enough, there's page after page of her well-styled selfies. Not a hint of Tanner. Not a hint of anything but her.

I do the same with Tim Wagner, but he's a better ghost than Dutch is. He truly is proving to be invisible.

My phone bleats, and I jump. It's a text from Noah.

Goodnight, Lottie. I love you.

"Aww." I can't help but show both Dutch and Pancake the screen. Neither of which is amused. I text right back.

Love you, too. Don't work too hard! I'm beginning to forget what you look like.

It doesn't take but three seconds for him to respond.

Believe me, honey. Once I frost your cookies, you will never forget me.

I let out a toe-curling squeal at the thought.

All night I dream of frosting cookies with Noah.

CHAPTER 8

"*B*azingas is on the wrong side of Leeds," I say as Everett, Dutch, and I stand outside the questionable establishment staring up at a forty-foot neon sign of a smiling woman holding a tray in which she rests her bazingas on. Each of the aforementioned bazingas lights up in a psychedelic array of purple and green.

"Every side of Leeds is the wrong side," Everett says, pressing his hand into the small of my back as we enter the raunchy restaurant.

"Preach it, brother," I say taking in the cantankerous crowd. The restaurant itself is brightly lit with booths and tables scattered about, rock music blares through the speakers, and despite the light snowfall outside, every waitress has donned a pair of jean cut-off shorts that technically qualify as a belt. An itty-bitty bikini top graces their amply endowed upper torsos, each side dotted with a purple star. And smashed over each one of their heads is a red sequin Santa hat. We've been wearing them down at the bakery as well, but not nearly as flashy.

"I'm not your brother," Everett whispers. "It's date night, remember?"

"That's right," I say, threading my arm through his. Everett and I thought we should come in with a story in the event someone asks questions. In the least we should be on the same deceptive page.

Dutch bounds around as if thrilled to be here. In truth, Dutch is always far too thrilled to be anywhere I take him—correction, anywhere he follows me. I'm guessing his exuberance has far less to do with the fact he's usually Rainbow Bridge bound and more to do with the fact he's exuberant by nature. I've never seen such a happy pet in all my life. Pancake is the anti-Dutch, always scowling and sleeping his days away. And in a twisted way, it's what I love most about him. Go figure.

A string of red garland garners my attention, affixed to a faux cardboard fireplace that's taped to the wall, and lining every inch of it are miniature stockings that bear a bevy of girls' names—one of which is Bella.

"Everett, look. She *does* work here." I point over just as a short brunette with an ear-to-ear grin comes up in her scantily clad uniform. Both her bazingas and that smile are pointed at Everett. Her nametag reads *Sugar*, and I can't help but scowl at her.

She giggles into him. "Well, aren't you a tall glass of eggnog. I bet you go down real smooth and easy."

Everett's chest rumbles with a dull laugh as I pull him in close.

"He's my eggnog." The words come out snippy, but I can't help it. He's not really, but a date night is involved. Besides, I don't like the way she's leering at him. It doesn't feel safe. "Table for two, please? In the non-boyfriend stealing section."

The tiny waitress openly growls at me before leading us to a booth near the back, which is perfect because it's an open view to the entire perverted place.

Dutch ambles over and hops up next to me, so I scoot over in an effort to make room for him.

"What are you doing?" Everett looks concerned at my decision to off-center myself from him.

"Dutch is joining us for dinner." I tick my head to my left where Dutch is lying down with his head perched over the side of the bench, as not to miss a moment of the bazinga action. He's such a boy.

"One more joining you?" Sugar perks to life once again. "I'll bring another plate setting."

We put in our drink orders, and she gives me the stink eye before taking off.

Everett grunts my way. "Way to get on her good side. If she spits on my hot wings, I may not forgive you."

"If she spits on your hot wings, it's because she's trying to cast a spell on you. She was practically hypnotized by your presence in the event you didn't notice, *Eggnog*."

His lids hood low, and a slippery grin glides over his lips for less than a second as he reaches over and picks up my hand.

"I like you jealous, Cupcake."

"Again with the Cupcake?"

"Yes. If you're my girlfriend, I'd like to gift you a nickname. Cupcake is cute and adorable. I think it's rather fitting."

"*Ooh?* Does that mean I've graduated to calling you Essex?"

"No." Any trace of a smile dissolves once again.

"Oh well. At least you can add me to your infamous exes' roster by the time we hit dessert."

Everett squints out his disapproval. "Think bigger, Lemon. You're worth it."

"I'm worth what?" I shake my head a moment before a thought comes to me. "Oh no! I ticked off the tiny two-timer, and now I bet she won't want to give up the goods on Bella! I don't even know if she's here tonight, but there's nothing like a scorned co-worker to give us the lowdown on our prime suspect. At least the prime suspect for now. You'll have to flirt with her. She'd give you the bikini right off her back in exchange for a sip of your holiday cheer."

"I'm not flirting with her. I'm not that kind of boyfriend."

"You picked a fine time to be loyal."

Dutch lifts his head my way, and I give him a quick scratch behind his ears.

"You're loyal, too," I coo. "Far more loyal than just about any other nonliving creature has ever been to me." I force a smile Everett's way. "Don't get excited. I wasn't complimenting you. I was talking to the dog."

"Geez, Lemon. We need to get to the bottom of this. Aren't there some people you can see about this problem? Don't they have a number people like you can call up to help work out the kinks? Isn't that what the psychic hotline is for?"

I can't help but scoff at my newly minted boyfriend—who, by the way, is still holding my hand. It's a bit sweet, actually.

"Let's get one thing straight, buddy. I'm no psychic. I'm a one hundred percent Honey Hollow hometown girl who cherishes good friends and knows her way around a kitchen. There's simply nothing special about me."

Dutch gives a friendly, warbling bark my way.

"I beg to differ." Everett gives my fingers a light squeeze. "I know that it's none of my business, Lemon, but I think you need to start digging into your biological family."

"It's Cupcake to you and a big, fat no to that bad idea. I am not digging into my biological family. Besides, they're a complete mystery to me. I wouldn't even know where to begin."

"Well, you're proving to be a darn good detective. I think if you put your mind to it you could pull it off in spades."

My heart wrenches at the thought. In truth, this time of year always makes me a little melancholy at the fact there's a family out there that rejected me. I know I shouldn't look at it that way, but I can't help it. There's a very real little girl who lives inside of me that insists on feeling a bit sorry for herself at the holidays.

"Speaking of detectives"—I'm quick to change the subject—"how are we going to get any info on Tanner's bodacious beauty?"

A thunderous applause erupts behind us as a flurry of Bazingas' finest all congregate around a table of teenage boys and break out into a cheery yet significantly altered version of "Happy Birthday," and when they're through, the entire crew shakes their bazingas.

Everett pulls my hand to his lips. "I'm having a brainstorm, Cupcake."

"I bet you are."

"Hey"—he dips his nose to my fingers—"you smell amazing. Like sugar and—"

"Cinnamon," I finish for him. "And you would too if you were baking up enough gingerbread boys and girls to conduct a hostile takeover of the living."

A shadow darkens the table, and we look up to see Noah Corbin Fox, stone-faced and yet vexingly handsome.

"What's going on?" He glowers at his former stepbrother a moment.

I pull my hand back like pulling it from a fire. "He was just sniffing my cookies!"

Noah's eyes light with fire sort of the way Dutch's do on a permanent basis.

The waitress comes by and sets another plate setting down next to Everett, and Noah takes a seat, those angry slits he sees the world through firmly focused on me.

"*Pardon me.*" Everett catches the waitress' attention before she has a chance to bounce away. "It's her birthday," he says, pointing my way, and I can't help but shoot him a dirty look. I bet he'd like for me to get bazingaed while he surveys the flesh buffet as if it were a choice dessert. So what if Bella is serenading us? I still don't see how I'm going to get her to out herself as a murderer—especially not in a crowd of her co-workers—especially not in a bikini top that hardly covers her bazingas.

Sugar scowls at me before taking our orders—one order of hot wings for Everett and two dittos from Noah and me.

"Great," I say once she takes off. "Now she's going to spit in all of our dinners." I glower at Noah. "Enjoying a quick dinner break? Or should I say quickie?"

His affect smooths out, and he's got that hot five o'clock shadow going on and those dimples are effortlessly digging in on their own free will. My word, this man never fails to slay me with his comeliness.

"I think we all know why we're here."

Everett nods to Noah. "Cupcake and I are enjoying a date night. Ivy meeting you here?"

Noah glances my way. "Very funny. And no. We thought it would be less suspicious if I came alone." His brows dip into a hard V. "Date night, really?"

"Yes, really," I say. "And you can thank us once all of those bodacious beauties come shaking their bazingas at me. I bet Bella will be one of them."

"So you know her name." Noah tips his head my way in a congratulatory manner. "I can appreciate the fact that you keep trying to interject yourself into a homicide investigation that you feel you have a personal connection with. I don't like it, but I can appreciate it." His features darken—also a vexingly sexy look on the man who has threatened to frost my cookies in the very near future. And, my stars, how my cookies are eager for that frosting. "But what I don't appreciate is the fact the two of you have once again found yourselves in a social orbit that consistently has a bad element to it."

I suck in a quick breath. "What? Believe you me, honey. Those women who work the strip clubs aren't doing it as an easy and effective way to meet impressive men. They're doing it because, more often than not, they have another mouth to feed, a much smaller one that was aggressively purged from their own body, i.e., children. And these girls here?" I blank a moment. "Okay, so some of them are hoping to meet impressive detectives and judges, but mostly their tips are out of this world. I should know. I earned a decent wage when I worked the tables at the Honey Pot Diner. And if they're earning triple what I was—well, if this baking gig doesn't pan out, I might just don a bikini myself. So as you can see, I'm not really a big fan of this chauvinistic conversation."

Noah's lids hang low. "I meant in this seedy part of town. In no way would I put down a woman for how she chooses to put bread on the table."

"Oh. Right." My cheeks burn with embarrassment for a moment. Nonetheless, a thought comes to me, and I excuse myself as I head for the restroom. Dutch hops alongside me as if I've suddenly decided to take him on an impromptu walk and in a way, I have.

I spot Sugar finishing up with a table near the entry and speed up just in time to bump into her.

"Oooh, sorry!" I help right the empty tray in her hand. "Say? Can I ask you a quick question?" I shuttle us to the corridor that leads to the restrooms. "Do you know Bella?"

She inches back before glancing to the floor. "Bells? She's here somewhere."

"Oh, right. Yeah, I thought I spotted her earlier." Liar, liar, Cupcake on fire. "I mean, she's an old friend of mine." Seriously? And she's here? I smell a not-so happy reunion if Sugar feels the need to reunite old friends, but something tells me she's not that interested in either of us. "She's been acting kind of strange lately. Did she just undergo a bad breakup or something?"

Sugar's berry-stained lips crimp as she pulls me deeper into the hall, a good sign of juicy tidbits to come. "You got that right. First, she found out that louse she was seeing was two-timing her with her dad's girlfriend—and, of course, he swore he'd never do it again. Then the idiot turns up dead. She's devastated. It's like the knife was plunged into her chest twice—and at Christmastime no less."

More like icicle. Appropriate, considering the fact Tanner was sort of cold-hearted.

"Her dad's girlfriend, huh?" The thought churns my stomach. Tanner's libido truly knew no bounds. "That's pretty low. No wonder she acts as if she doesn't even know me." Ha! Perfect cover!

"Tell me about it. She's been walking around here like a zombie for the last few days. You'd think she offed the guy herself." She takes off as I struggle to catch my breath. My goodness, Bella Carter could just be the one who did it!

I head back to the table in time to see a literal cupcake floating toward it as an entire gaggle of scantily clad girls bounce their bazingas my way. The clapping is far too loud, the song is amazingly obnoxious, and both Noah and Everett look as if they need a glass of ice water flung in their faces. But I'm far too mesmerized by the redhead with the oversized eyes. Her face is puffy, and her affect isn't nearly as cheery as the rest of the crowd. Not only does her nametag give away the fact it's Bella—the fact I clearly recognize her from the night of the Christmas party cinches the deal. The waitresses shake their bazingas at Noah and Everett before disappearing back to the four corners of the establishment. But I spot Bella heading toward the same corridor I just cornered Sugar in.

"Enjoy the cupcake, boys," I say to Noah and Everett before Dutch and I head off on mission number two. Hey? Who knew having a double date with Noah and Everett would bring me such incredible luck? And I don't mean double date in the traditional sense. Suffice it to say, I feel a little smug to be in a place like this with my own male harem.

"Excuse me," I say and Bella turns around, stunningly beautiful with perfect porcelain skin, eyes that glitter like black diamonds. "Uh—" Great. What now? I look down and note I'm holding a napkin. "I think you dropped this." I hold it out between us, and she makes a face before swiping it from my hand.

"Thank you." She sniffles as if she were one misplaced napkin away from losing it.

"Whoa, hey." I sling my arm around her shoulders. "It's not the end of the world. I used to be a waitress, too. And, believe you me, I know all about wanting to get the job done right."

Tears spout from her. "It has nothing to do with work, believe me." She dabs her eyes with the cloth napkin I just handed over. "In fact, I shouldn't even be here."

"Boy trouble?" I don't see why we shouldn't get right down to brass tacks.

She nods. "As in past tense. Let's just say it didn't end well."

"Relationships with jerks never do." My word, I pray she saw Tanner for who he really was.

"Oh, he wasn't a jerk. Not until the end anyway. We were going to run off and get married. He bought me a ring and everything."

"Really? A real ring or one of those candy ones you pick up in a gumball machine?" Inquiring minds really do want to know.

A small laugh chortles from her. "It's very nice of you to try to make me feel better, but I really should get back out there." She makes a face at the crowded restaurant.

"I get it. But just know that no man is worth those tears. I'm sure you'll find someone else far better suited for you."

She shakes her head emphatically, those dark eyes glossy and stained with crimson tracks. "No way. I'll be steering clear of relationships for a good long while. It was ugly, and let's just say it brought out an ugly side in me that I really didn't expect. Not to mention the fact my brother went ballistic as soon as he found out. Things took a very nasty turn." She shudders, and Dutch barks right at her as she takes off down the hall.

"Hey?" I bend over and give him a scratch under the chin, and those blazing red eyes heat right into mine. "Is she the killer? Is that why you're barking?"

He whimpers and looks unreasonably sad, and for whatever reason it doesn't instill a whole lot of confidence in me.

I head back to the table and tell Noah and Everett what I've gleaned from both Sugar and Bella.

Noah nods. "I think we might have found our girl."

I glance to Dutch and twist my lips. "I don't know. A part of me still thinks something isn't adding up. It can't really be that easy, right? I mean, she practically confessed to me, a stranger of all people."

Everett shrugs. "That's not unusual. It helps the perpetrator get it off their chest with no real consequences. I'm betting she feels better just by speaking with you."

The loyal pooch by my side lets out a series of ear-piercing howls and growls.

"Dutch!" I call out in fear he'll not only wake the dead but invoke the curiosity of the living as well.

ADDISON MOORE

"Dutch?" Noah leans in, his eyes tracing my hand as I quickly realize I was absentmindedly stroking the yippy puppy's back.

"Dutch?" I look to Everett for help.

"Yes, dutch," he says, pulling out his wallet. "As in we all pay for our own meal. I like how you think, Lemon. For a second I thought I'd have to foot his bill, too."

I try to throw some money into the pot, and Noah gently pushes it away.

"My treat, Lot."

We head out into the icy December air, and Noah wraps an arm around me. "Thank you, Lottie. I don't think I could have gotten nearly as much info on my own. Ivy may not like it, but I'm glad you were here." He lands a heated kiss to my lips, and we linger as Everett clears his throat. "I've got to head back to the station."

"I know," I whisper as we hug it out, and I offer another far juicier kiss to his lips.

"Goodnight," he says to the both of us before pinning a threatening look to Everett. "You stay away from her cookies."

"Will do." Everett mock salutes him as Noah hops into his truck and takes off.

Everett and I circle around the parking lot, and my eyes snag on a white Toyota Corolla that looks as if it's seen better days—specifically on that dent on its front end.

"Everett!" I sing his name in a panic as I point over to it.

"Holy smokes." He heads over and pulls out his phone, taking several pictures of the incriminating dent. "I'll shoot these to you." He crouches on his knees as he gives it a closer inspection. "Look here, there's a streak of dark paint. It looks like this could very well be the car we've been looking for."

"So, Bella really might be the killer?"

Dutch howls at the moon as if he were about to morph into a werewolf.

"Hush, you!" I hiss as Everett straightens.

"I take it Dutch doesn't agree?"

"Maybe. Or maybe he's just really happy to see it's a full moon?"

Everett wraps an arm around my shoulders as we head to his car. "Let's get this information to Noah so he can button up this case by Christmas. You have a calendar to fill, Cupcake, remember?"

"You do realize I have no desire to talk about my sex life with you."

"Why not? We're dating."

We share a warm laugh as we pile into his car, with Dutch sprawling out over the back seat as we make our way back to Honey Hollow.

Bella Carter—murderer at large. Something about it doesn't sit right with me, and it has nothing to do with Dutch's strange behavior.

Bella Carter mentioned her brother went ballistic.

Maybe, just maybe, he went ballistic enough to kill.

oney Hollow Covenant Church is a boxy building encased in white bricks and attached firmly to its side is Carlson Hall, the destination for most after-funeral affairs, and this is the second of which occasions I've been asked to cater. The first time I was asked it was by poor Collette Jenner's mother, and this time my own mother reached out on behalf of the church. Of course, I felt it was bad decorum to make an appearance in the actual service, but seeing that my cookies are on order, I'm sticking around for the after-party.

The hall is bustling with bodies, mostly gorgeous females that one might consider romantic contenders for the deceased, and why does this not surprise me?

As soon as I arrived, Dutch took off running into the hall, acting as if I never let him off his spiritual leash anymore. Last night he curled his handsome self around Pancake as if he were protecting his new furry friend, and it warmed my heart. Pancake shockingly slept right through the carnage.

Everett helped me schlep my cookies from the new van he bought me. It's still my very favorite toy—the van, not Everett. Last month, I was actually competing to win a refrigerated van for the bakery but ended up catching Collette's killer and restoring Everett's good name. He felt he owed me, but it couldn't be further from the truth. As for delivering the cookies this afternoon, I could have done it all by my lonesome, but Everett assured me he did not want me mingling with a potential murderer on my own. It's *potentially* true. I'm willing to bet money the murderer is here.

I'm also willing to bet Noah and Ivy will show up at some point, but so far I haven't spotted them.

"Lottie!" Mother chirps as she heads on over with none other than her brand new boy toy leashed to her side. And knowing what I do about Brad Rutherford's kinky preferences, that might as well have been a literal statement.

"Brace yourself," I whisper to Everett. "She's coming in hot."

"Oh, Lottie." Mom lunges at me with a hug. "I know how hard this must be for you. Standing in a room full of people who assume you're guilty of murder!"

"Actually, the thought never crossed my mind." I pull back and look to Mr. Rutherford. "I see the two of you are still running in the same social circles."

He belts out a hearty laugh, and sadly half the room is doing just that so it doesn't seem that out of character. "I promise I'm treating your mother like the queen she is." He looks to her and waggles his brows. "Her wish is my command."

"Gross," I mutter.

Everett touches his shoulder to mine. "It's nice to see you've recovered so well." He nods to my mother's plus one. "I would be devastated if I learned that my wife were trying to poison me."

Ha! Take that, Brad the cad.

Mr. Rutherford's chest expands, and my mother is quick to wrap her arms around him as if he were bloating with helium and about to float to the ceiling.

"Yes, well"—he looks tenderly down at my mother—"Miranda here has been a healing balm." She coos up at him appreciatively. "Apply twice daily and rub vigorously!"

The two of them break out into a fit of laughter as they stagger off into the crowd.

"I'm going to vomit now." No sooner do I announce my intentions than Lainey traipses up with a Tanner lookalike that sends my adrenaline skyrocketing. The last thing you expect to see at a funeral is the deceased waltzing around dressed to kill in a three-piece suit. That is clearly Everett's department. And then it hits me. It's not Tanner at all that I'm staring at.

"Hook!" I wrap my arms around my old friend and pull back to admire him. Hook is Tanner's older, wiser, and far more handsome brother. If Lainey really wanted to make Forest insane, she sure snagged the wrong Redwood brother. Hook isn't really his formal name, but come to think of it, I've never known him by anything else, so maybe it is?

"Lottie Lemon. You look killer." He gives a sly wink. "Don't worry. I don't think you really slaughtered my brother." He shakes his head as he looks to Everett. "You must be Lottie's plus one. Hook Redwood."

"Everett Baxter."

"He's not my plus one. He's my plus one's ex-stepbrother. It's a long story. What's new with you? I hear you're turning the stock market on its ear. You're not the reason we're in a downswing, are you?" I tease.

Hook belts out a laugh, and half the eligible girls in the room turn to look this way. Honestly, half of them are swooning in Everett's direction, and this doesn't surprise me one bit.

"I'm doing all right. But now that Tanner is gone, I'll be relocating to Honey Hollow for the foreseeable future."

"Oh?" Lainey glances my way. "Why's that?"

A huge sigh expels from him. "I hope you won't think less of my father, but he wanted one of his sons to take over the family business." He looks to Everett. "My parents own Redwood Realty."

"Oh, I forgot about that," I say, wondering if the plot to Tanner's murder just thickened.

"That's right." Hook takes in the crowd. "We've got offices in Honey Hollow, Hollyhock, Leeds, and three in Ashford. My sister —Rachel, thankfully isn't too interested in having anything to do with the working end of the business. She's perfectly content collecting a check for now." He looks to Lainey. "She's expecting."

"That's great!" Lainey brightens. I remember that Tanner dragged Lainey off to her wedding a few months back. "Congratulations. You're going to be an uncle."

"And I very much look forward to it. I always thought I'd be married with children at this stage in my life. And I'm anxious to get there. I'm just sorry my goof of a brother won't be here to see it."

Everett leans in. "So you're taking over the family business. Is your father retiring?"

Way to keep him on track, Everett. I nudge my shoulder to his.

Hook looks forlorn over the fact. "I'm afraid so. And I hate to say a bad thing about my brother, especially considering the venue, but it's for the best the business lands in my hands." He gives Lainey the side eye. "No offense, but my brother couldn't keep his pants up long enough to sell a pencil, let alone an entire house."

Lainey's eyes bug out. "I think I see Rachel! I'll go congratulate her now." And just like that, our circle grows smaller.

"I've heard rumors about that whole couldn't keep his pants up thing." I make a face at Hook. And I've seen evidence, but I leave that tidbit out. "You don't think a disgruntled ex offed him, do you?" As bad as I feel for doing so, I had to ask. It practically begged the question.

Hook gives a soft chuckle. "My brother had no exes. He would sooner stab himself in the neck with an icicle than dump a girl. He was a lover, not a fighter."

Everett doesn't look amused, but then again, he never does. "So, you're saying this entire room is filled with prospective suspects."

Hook casts a quick glance around as he surveys the room. "I suppose so. But it would take a lot of rage to pull it off. I just can't see him getting anyone that worked up."

That trio of suspects Pete fed us the other night comes to mind. "A woman scorned could easily do it. So could a disgruntled co-worker with an axe to grind." Kelly Ferdinand comes to mind. I still don't know one iota about her. "Or a brother looking to close in on a real estate empire," I tease. But Hook drops that friendly grin from his face and stalks off.

Everett steps in close. "What did you do that for? You practically accused him of murder at his own brother's funeral."

"I had no idea he'd take it that way. Hook and I have always had an upbeat relationship. I guess I crossed a line."

"Or hit a nerve. Is that demon dog anywhere to be seen?"

"Dutch is not a demon. In fact, his ruby red eyes are quite enchanting once you get used to them. He's perfectly angelic when you get down to it. But no"—I crane my neck and spot him at the refreshment table—"right now he's trying to polish off a tray of oatmeal raisin cookies. It's my fault. I used that vanilla icing that drives him wild."

An older woman walks in front of us waving at someone behind Everett. "It was nice seeing you, Tim. And watch your packages. The thieves are still at it!" She waves again as she heads over to a familiar looking man with an unfortunately familiar looking dummy by his side. Ned Sweeny. I shudder just thinking about him and that stack of stupid perched on his arm who holds the key to my every living nightmare. Why would anyone play with those things willingly? What was the dummy's name again? Earl Gray? *Darjeeling*. That's right.

Everett taps my arm, waking me from my stupor. "That must be Tim Wagner." He glances to a younger man, early twenties, helping himself to one of my Christmas spritzer cookies. There's something familiar about him I can't quite place.

"You're right!" I yank Everett along without putting another thought into it. "Oh, hey," I say to the young man as I reach for a couple of gingerbread cookies myself. "Sad day," I say, looking right at him. "How did you know poor Tanner?"

"Poor Tanner." He averts his eyes as if he were anything but. "I worked with the guy." He gives a quick glance over his shoulder. "He got me fired a few weeks back, so he wasn't exactly my favorite person."

"Fired? Whatever for?" So it's true. Ha! Good old Pete really was a wealth of information.

He waves it off as he crunches a stack of iced sugar cookies into his mouth. "You know, everyone at the Parks and Recs Department takes off midday and puts down five on the time card. It's a known fact. But it was just an excuse to get rid of me." He pops another cookie into his mouth, and I shrug to Everett as if asking for help.

Everett picks up a dessert plate and neatly piles on a nice mound of cookies himself. "So, what was the real reason?" Everett has a calm, trusting demeanor about him. He could wrangle even the most delicate secret out of anyone, and twice as easily if that anyone happens to be female.

Tim surveys the room and scoffs as his gaze stops short of a stunning brunette with a pixie cut, and I gasp at the sight of her. That's her! The last and final woman who had a chance to carnally climb Mount Redwood—at least that I'm aware of. Tanner could have had fifty by the time he ran out the door and was slaughtered. The boy had moves.

"He didn't like that I knew certain things about that family."

"Oh my goodness." I lean in. "What did you know?" Not one ounce of me wants to believe that Hook offed his brother so he could leave Wall Street to peddle Honey Hollow real estate.

He shakes his head as he looks back to Everett and me. "You really want to know? Ask Kelly Ferdinand yourself." He pops another cookie into his mouth before heading out into the snowy afternoon. And then it hits me where I've seen him before. He was the guy I thought looked a lot like Noah the night of Tanner's murder. He was in that small crowd that Lainey introduced us to. Huh. I turn to look at the pixie-haired brunette.

"That must be her."

We speed over just as Kelly and her adorable pixie cut are headed for the door.

"Excuse me!" I say, trying to slow her down.

She turns as she's cinching her coat before heading into the elements. "I'm sorry. I have a client in a few minutes, and I'm already running dreadfully behind." She looks from me to Everett. "Were the two of you looking for an appointment?"

"Yes," I quickly volunteer the two of us for whatever services she might be offering.

"Here." She riffles through her purse and stuffs a card into my hand. "Call anytime," she says as she stalks out the door.

Everett and I glance to the card, and our heads inch back at the very same time.

What in the world would Tanner Redwood need from someone like Kelly Ferdinand?

And what in the world are Everett and I going to do with her?

CHAPTER 10

*E*verett and I stand outside an office building in Leeds, yes, Leeds. And yes, it's just that bad. We're both dressed like consummate professionals, which took zero effort on his part and one hundred percent effort on mine. But in my defense, I felt compelled to look somewhat equally yoked to the good judge in hopes Ms. Ferdinand will buy our act. Something tells me it will be a little harder to pull the wool over her eyes than it was Bella and the bikini brigade. In my hands, I hold a box of warm Christmas crinkle cookies because really? I wasn't quite sure what cookies went best with what's about to happen behind those walls.

"Lemon," Everett says as we stare down the sign that proudly reads *Kelly Ferdinand, M.D. Sexual Therapist.*

Dutch whimpers as if he too were gravely concerned as to where this might lead next.

"I know, I know," I hiss. "But I swear this will be the very last time."

"It most assuredly will," a stern voice belts out from behind.

Everett and I turn to find Noah and Ivy Fairbanks dressed in matching hunter green wool coats, and I gasp at the coordinated fashion malfeasance. Noah's eyes are hooded low, his face stony, and the muscles in his jaw popping with aggression as he stares down Everett. That wide chest, those hands that look as if they're twitching to wring his ex-stepbrother's neck, Noah is one hundred percent man, and he just so happens to be my man.

"Oh no, you don't," I say, pulling Noah over to my side of the sexual divide. "Detective Fairbanks, consider yourself dismissed."

"Dismissed?" Her perfectly penciled in brows hike a notch as if she were amused. "What exactly are you dismissing me from? My own investigation? That's right, Carlotta. This investigation belongs to me."

My blood boils ten times more than before once she eschews my preferred moniker.

"You, Detective Fairbanks, may tend to whatever case you wish," I grit it through my teeth. "But where I draw the line is you sashaying into that office with my boyfriend attached to your side. I'm not sorry to break it to you, but there will be no faux bae, boo, or honey bear parade for you today. The investigation may belong to you, but Noah Corbin Fox belongs to me. You can keep your corpses. I've got a living, breathing, real man by my side."

I clasp my hand around Noah's and give a violent squeeze.

Ivy smirks my way. "Fine. Judge Baxter, would you kindly portray my paramour?"

"No," I snip without fully thinking it through. "He's mine, too." I pen him in with my elbow lest I drop my Christmas crinkles at my feet. "We are a happy threesome, and we're about to share that delicate information with the good doctor—with whom we are late for an appointment. So, if you'll excuse us, we need to get a move on."

She shoots venom with Noah. My goodness, Ivy Fairbank's eyes are far more frightening than Dutch's eyes could ever hope to be.

She sniffs the air in Noah's direction. "I'll have dinner waiting back at the office." She stalks off in her four-inch heels, and I can't help but note the red soles of those shoes are alerting me to the fact they cost more than my hatchback is worth.

Noah cuts a look to Everett. "Leave."

"Nope." Everett brings the lethal attitude right back at him. "Cupcake and I are here to learn a few party tricks to add to our repertoire."

My mouth falls open but not a word comes out because that just so happens to be the story we concocted in the car ride over.

A strange rumbling sound comes from deep within Noah's chest, and I'm half-afraid he's about to blow a hole right through Everett's skull.

"Again with the Cupcake?" Noah's chest expands like an accordion. "Don't you dare call her that. This Cupcake belongs to me."

Everett slings his arm around my shoulders in a clear act of defiance, and Noah's nostrils flare in a hot yet dangerous way.

"We're late, boys," I say, opening the door and hitching my head for them to follow along. "You're both coming with me."

Inside the office is homey with dense blue carpeting on the floor and a mahogany desk sits unmanned. Christmas carols play softly from the speakers, and a corner of the waiting area is decorated with a small stark white tree with cherry red bulbs. We're about to take a seat when the door to our left opens and the stunning brunette with her perky pixie cut wave us in.

"My secretary is off on holiday. She flew out to California to spend Christmas in the sun, so I apologize if you had to wait."

"Your timing is perfect," I assure her as we head on in, and Everett sits to my left and Noah to my right. Dutch spins in a small circle in the corner and promptly falls asleep. He doesn't seem to be having any adverse reaction to her, but I'm not entirely sure that clears her as the killer.

"Please"—she sits behind her enormous black lacquered desk, and I can't help but wonder what kinds of things have taken place in it, how many people have bent over it—"introduce yourselves."

"I'm Lo—Lolita and these are my, um, boyfriends—Essex and, um, Corbin." They're all partial truths. But seriously? *Lolita*? I could have done so much better had I not been under pressure.

A friendly laugh bubbles from her. "I assure you all I don't judge anyone, and I certainly won't judge the three of you. You'd be surprised how many polyamorous relationships I've come across."

Everett clicks his shoe to mine. "Leeds."

"Pardon?" She perks to life in his direction. "Yes, please tell me anything you'd like me to know about you and your situation. We'll start with you, Essex. When did you realize that Lolita was the one for you?"

A dark laughs brews in his chest. "The day she fell to her knees and knocked her head to my crotch."

Noah explodes with a violent cough that I'm afraid will morph into a violent fistfight. Sadly, Everett didn't have to fabricate a word.

"We ran into each other quite literally," I'm quick to say as I look to Noah. "It's the truth." And for the life of me, I can't remember if I ever shared anything about the salacious meet and greet I had with his stepbrother the first day we met. I suppose the crotch-thumping cat is out of the bag now. I take a moment to scowl at Everett.

The good doctor looks to Noah. "And how did you meet Lolita? Was it an equally colorful introduction?"

Noah's lips lift on one end, and I shrink a little in my seat. "Yes, Dr. Ferdinand, it was equally colorful." His eyes flit my way, and my heart skips a solid beat. "She bounced into my office, and after a brief verbal exchange, we too found ourselves in a tussle. I believe there was a generous lending of delicate body parts, and for a while I believed that perhaps she was flirting with me. But now I see that Lolita here simply has a propensity for physical altercations."

I shrink down in my seat a little bit more. It would be just my luck to need more therapy for my relationship after I leave this office than I needed when I stepped in.

"Corbin"—she twists a pen between her fingers—"what, if any, sexual pressures do you feel within the relationship?"

Everett grunts in lieu of a laugh. "They haven't hit the sheets yet. They've decided to pencil it in, and life hasn't allowed for that to happen."

"Pencil it in?" Kelly here looks equally as disturbed by this as Everett did when he first found out. And why is penciled in sex so bad to begin with?

"All good ideas start with a plan," I point out.

"I agree," Noah pipes up, that threatening stare slow to disengage from Everett. He looks to Dr. Ferdinand. "Lot—*Lolita* and I are quite eager to take our relationship to the next level."

She shakes her head as if maybe we're not. "I'm sorry, but I'm not buying it. Not a lot of men would schedule a first-time encounter or agree to keep it dropping down the calendar. I'm thinking this has more to do with your insecurity with her relationship with Essex." She looks to Everett. "I'm assuming the two of you have consummated your relationship?"

"Yes." Everett doesn't miss a coital beat. "Many, many satisfying times."

Noah huffs a dull laugh. "If she's so satisfied, then why is she looking forward to having me frost her cookies?"

I give a frenetic nod to Everett. "Yes, Essex. I very much look forward to having Corbin frost my cookies."

Everett's lids hood low, and the slight hint of a smile rides on his lips. "Nobody could ever frost your cookies the way I can, Cupcake."

Noah and Everett engage in an escalating war of salty words, and the room feels as if it's spinning. Dr. Ferdinand's lips are moving, and I can't turn my head left and right fast enough to keep up with the madness, so I simply turn around as far as I can only to spot a sofa behind us and sitting upon it are the prying eyes of a—

A scream rips from me, and the room goes quiet as all eyes fall to the wooden menace watching us attentively with his legs comfortably crossed.

Dr. Ferdinand trills with laugher. "Please don't mind Charlie. He was gifted to me by one of my dear clients."

"Client?" The creepy dummy that Ned Sweeny insists on dragging around with him at Christmas parties and funerals alike comes to mind. I turn back to Kelly Ferdinand. "Ned Sweeny?"

Her eyes triple in size, and she doesn't have to say a word.

"I'm sorry, Lolita. I'm not allowed to disclose my clients' names. But if you find the puppet disturbing, I can have it removed."

"Oh no, that's fine." I glance to Everett and Noah. "I was just taken by surprise. The arguing didn't help the matter." A thought comes to me. "It just reminded me of a relationship I had that ended badly. Have you ever had a relationship end badly?" Finally. A segue that leads right back to Tanner.

"No." She shakes her head as if it were an impossibility.

Drats.

"Oh, wait." She grimaces. "Yes, actually and quite recently at that."

"How did it end, if you don't mind me asking?"

"Not at all." Her brows furrow as if she minded very much. "Let's just say for as much one-on-one time we enjoyed—it was necessary for us to take a permanent vacation." A devious smile lifts her lips. "Although, before I could relay that news, he came to other, unforeseen circumstances and we indeed ended rather abruptly."

"Any hard feelings?"

Her mouth opens a moment, then closes just like that creepy marionette is probably doing behind our backs.

"No hard feelings whatsoever. In fact, you might say I'm a bit relieved."

Relieved? My entire body goes rigid.

She squints over at the three of us. "Why don't we wrap it up for today? I like to finish up on a positive note. Essex, why don't you say something nice about your relationship with Lolita."

Everett's chest expands as he turns to me, and Dr. Ferdinand shakes her head.

"No, no, I'm a firm believer in physical contact. Please stand and hold her as you pour your affection for her. Take a moment and envision the things you'd like to do to her the next time the two of you are intimate. Look her in the eyes as you envision your bodies intertwined. Envision how much pleasure you plan on invoking in her. Envision—"

"Don't do it," Noah lays the words out like a tangible threat.

Everett gives me a hand and pulls me in close, his hands riding up and down my back in a figure eight, and I scowl up at him because I happen to know he's putting on a show just to get a rise out of Noah. Thank goodness I don't have to face Noah —just yet.

"Go ahead, Essex"—Dr. Ferdinand is quick to cheer him on—"tell Lolita how she makes you feel. Look deep into her eyes as you visualize the two of you in the throes of passion."

A slow blooming grin threatens to break out on Everett's face, but he tempers it. His virility radiates off him in waves.

"Lolita"—his lips rubber band in the world's quickest, world's dirtiest smile—"you have been nothing but a bright light in my life." His gaze drills into mine, and his words feel heartfelt and genuine. "And when we're alone, naked in my bed—"

My face heats fifty degrees, and I'm pretty certain I'm about to combust. I'm pretty certain Noah is about to combust, too.

Noah coughs so loud it sounds as if a grenade just detonated behind me.

Everett's brows hike a notch. "The things you do to me—with that mouth"—he touches his finger to my lips a moment—"I'm pretty sure they're illegal in all fifty states." Another dark laugh strums from his chest. "But none of them compare to the things I'm going to do to you tonight." He shoots a wicked look to Noah.

"Bravo!" Dr. Ferdinand breaks out into spontaneous applause. "That was very impassioned. Why don't you tie a nice neat bow on it? You should kiss her."

"You should not kiss," Noah booms dangerously insistent.

But Everett only tightens his grip on me, his head cocked with devilish delight. "Sorry, buddy, doctor's orders." He leans in and brushes a chaste kiss just shy of my lips. But, unfortunately, Noah can't see that. Everett moans his way through it like the insolent brute he is. "Delicious." He pulls back and nods to Noah. "Give it your best shot."

I take a deep breath before turning to Noah. His feet are set in a defiant stance, his head tipped down, still shooting Everett with those death rays before he softens and reverts his attention to me. Noah's lips twitch with a barely-there smile, his lids hood destructively low, and there's not a question about the fact he's bedroom eyeing me.

"Lot"—Noah wraps his arms lovingly around me, and I melt into his embrace—"since the day I met you, I've known there was something special about you. And after that first kiss we shared, I knew you were the one for me, not just for the present, but for the future, too." He bears into the words, enunciating hard, and every cell in my body dissolves with pleasure. "When we finally get a chance to take our relationship to that special place"—he dots my lips with a kiss, and my heart explodes on cue—"and we will very, very soon—I will blow doors off anything Essex has ever dreamed of doing to you. And I'm beginning to think you're a nightly visitor in his nocturnal wanderings." He shoots the death rays over my shoulder once again. "I love you, Lot. You're my everything."

"Beautiful! Beautiful!" Dr. Ferdinand is on her feet, her applause far more boisterous than it was before.

Noah leans in and kisses me with all his heart, all his soul, and every unchaste intention he might be harboring.

And I wholeheartedly approve of all three.

We take off and wait until we're sealed on the other side of the office door before we pause a moment.

Everett lifts his chin my way. "What's next, Lemon?"

Noah growls audibly. "You take a cold shower—and for the love of all things holy, do not envision what you would like to do to her body."

"Actually"—I look to the two of them and sigh—"there is another man I'm interested in seeing, and his name is Ned Sweeny."

CHAPTER 11

*W*hen assembling gingerbread houses, one must have equal parts patience and equal parts faith it will all work out in the end. It takes a steady hand, a little trial and error, and a mountain of royal icing to accomplish the feat. Not to mention copious amounts of time considering the fact the Cutie Pie Bakery and Cakery is putting together close to twenty of these candied wonders a day.

By the time the bakery closes, my feet move slow as molasses, ironically, and my body feels as if I used it as a rolling pin for the last ten hours. But there's no hope of cuddling up with Dutch and Pancake in the next hour. In fact, the next few hours aren't looking so good either. It's the night of Honey Hollow's official tree lighting ceremony, and the entire town has congregated en mass just down the street. I had the crew deliver dozens of cookie platters for the event about an hour ago. It felt good crossing another huge holiday order off my list.

The Cutie Pie Bakery has really taken off like a sugar-fueled rocket, and I couldn't be happier about it. I couldn't be more exhausted either. I've yet to take a day off, unless you count Thanksgiving. And considering I cooked and cleaned all day, I'm not too sure it counted.

I walk over with the ever-faithful Dutch by my side. His glowing red eyes add yet another spark of holiday cheer to Main Street, which is lit up with a million twinkle lights. Dozens of carolers are dressed up like Dickens' characters, and the local elementary school has a booth set up selling both hot cocoa and steaming cups of cider.

As soon as I hit the festivities, Dutch begins to run circles around the masses as if people were his new favorite toy, and I'm betting they are, *were*.

I spot my mother and Mr. Rutherford cozied up near the enormous evergreen, which stands like a dark shadow just waiting for its grand entry into our holiday season. Just past the enormous three-tiered fountain that sits in the middle of Town Square are dozens of miniature trees that will be lit up as well, transforming our rather plain town into a bona fide winter wonderland.

"Lottie!" a cheerful male voice resounds from behind, and I turn to find Noah closing in on me, his arms around my waist, his lips pressed to mine before I can greet him. "Hey, beautiful." He pulls back with a dreamy look on his face that disappears as quick as it came. "Where's Everett?"

"Not with me. I don't make it a practice to keep tabs on him either." I peck a kiss to his lips before my own mood sours. "Where's Ivy? Does she know you escaped Ashford?"

"Very funny." He takes up my hand as we move over to the hundred-year-old oak the town has nicknamed Nelson. "I'm actually doing a little investigating tonight. Just looking to see if I note anything."

"Hit a dead end, huh?"

"I'm not proud to say it."

"If it makes you feel better, I'm in the same place."

"No"—a short-lived laugh bounces from his chest—"it most certainly does not make me feel better. In fact, it makes me feel worse to know you're inserting yourself into a potentially dangerous situation. Let me handle this."

"But the sooner we track down Tanner's killer, the sooner we can get to the business of being alone for a prolonged period of time. Besides, two heads are better than one."

"I agree." He pulls my hand up and kisses the tip of my finger. "And that's exactly why Detective Fairbanks and I are working overtime to make sure that happens."

"I wasn't talking about that head, and I seriously doubt she's interested in our love life."

"No, but she's interested in who the killer is." He touches his forehead to mine. "*I* am very much interested in our love life. And I'm going to make certain it's a good one, healthy, frequently tended to, and exceptionally creative."

"Creative? I like that." A bubbling laugh escapes me. I'm just about to say something equally salacious when a couple of figures near the fountain garner my attention. "Hey, isn't that Dr. Ferdinand and Ned Sweeny?" I suck in a quick breath once I spot that wooden malfeasance. "It is! He's got that repulsive piece of pine dangling from his limb like an extra appendage. I still can't get over the fact that Dr. Ferdinand said she was relieved over Tanner's death. I mean, who says that?"

"Someone who's glad he isn't around anymore—if indeed she was talking about him."

Noah and I watch as the two of them engage in a pretty heated conversation. Ned picks up Dr. Ferdinand's hand and gives it a tug, but she pulls away and takes off.

A spotlight is thrust near the tree and lands on a rather cheerful Mayor Nash.

"Good evening, residents and visitors alike. Welcome to our annual tree lighting ceremony. We are thrilled to have you as a part of the celebration." He drones on, but I can't seem to stop following Ned Sweeny with my eyes as he struggles to navigate his way through the crowd.

I give Noah's facial scruff a soft scratch. "That ended badly, wouldn't you say?"

"Agree. But it doesn't necessarily mean anything." He scans the area as if looking for Dr. Ferdinand.

The crowd chants backward from ten and we join.

"Three, two, one—" I leap in Noah's arms as our world explodes with a million colorful lights. "It's magic!" I cry as I steal a kiss and Noah steals one right back, his lips conforming over mine with a fire all their own. They say *things between us are about to get exceptionally creative*. They say *I own you*—and he does in the very worst way.

A piercing whistle goes off across the way, and we look up to find Ivy waving Noah over.

"Good Lord"—I mutter—"it's as if she senses we're together and she's determined to put an end to our good time. She's rather creative herself."

Noah groans, "I'd better go see what this is about."

"I'll give you the long and short of it. It's about her keeping you from me. She might throw in a conversation about those package thefts because I seriously doubt she has a lead on Tanner's killer."

"Funny. But an impossible feat for anyone to keep me from you." He takes off just as Ned Sweeny and that creepy wooden toddler he keeps with him pass me by.

"Ned!" I say brightly as if we were old friends and he pauses a moment, his own features smoothing out into an affable expression. "Just thought I'd say hello to Darjeeling." Liar, liar, I'd rather set my hair on fire. True story.

"Sure thing," he says just as Dutch bounds our way and, oh my word, it looks as if he's about to leap—"*Oof.*" Ned takes a stagger step forward. Right through him. Wow. Good Show, Dutch. Good show. "My goodness, it's as if a breeze just came out of nowhere." He gives a nervous laugh as he straightens the dummy, and the wooden monster's eyes and mouth move at once.

"Hello there, young lady," Darjeeling's wooden teeth clatter.

A dull laugh pumps through me. "He's so charming. Do you ever leave the house without him?"

"Just for work, but I like to make sure he's out and about at festive occasions such as this. It gives the children such joy to see him."

What Ned calls joy others call nightmares. I note the fact their suits are matching again, different from the checkered ones they wore the night of that disastrous holiday party.

"Your suits, they match." I try to sound cheery and not creeped out at all by the fact.

"Oh yes. I am meticulous about it. In fact, we have a dozen or so that go together. My father and my grandfather were also ventriloquists. I have quite the collection in my downstairs study. If you ever find yourself up for an afternoon of inquisitive fun, you should stop by sometime. We're the last house up on Farmington Way."

"That's not too far from me at all. I might just take you up on that someday. Um, you said *we?*"

"My wife and I. Hannah Carter and I married a few years back. Perhaps you know her?"

I shake my head, drawing a blank.

"You probably know Bella and Mason. My stepchildren."

"Bella!" I catch myself off guard as her name flies from my lips. "Yes, I believe we've met." Mason must be the brother she mentioned that had a knack for going berserk on her behalf. It's a miracle she still works at Bazingas if that's really the case.

"In fact, I'm in a bit of a hurry. My wife is a little under the weather, and I was just about to pick up some soup for her."

"Your wife." I nod, stunned by this matrimonial tidbit. "Well, I hope she feels better soon," I say, walking to the curb with him. That's right, he did mention he was married with two children the night of Tanner's murder. That entire night was a bit overwhelming it's no wonder I can't keep the details straight.

We part ways, and I watch as he jumps into a dark navy minivan and straps Darjeeling in as if he were a child.

"So weird," I say it lower than a whisper.

Ned waves my way as he waits for a crowd to pass before him. I take a step forward, my hand lifted in the air, and I freeze as I see it. A rather impressive dent just above the broken taillight in the back. Two white lines streak over the paint next to the busted taillight like lightning.

I take in a lungful of iced December air as he takes off.

So it was his car that Bella Carter hit. It had to be. It makes sense. They were both at the community center that night. I bet he's well aware of who hit him since they're both in the same family. Weird coincidence though.

I watch as he struggles to navigate his way down a street full of people and wonder what it all means.

CHAPTER 12

*W*inter has spread her wings over Honey Hollow, turning the entire tiny town into a virtual icebox. By the time I closed up the bakery, it felt as if I had stepped out into a snow globe with the lights, the carolers, and the virtual powdered sugar falling softly from the sky. Thick crowds stormed Main Street, clutching packages in one hand, steaming cocoa in the other, and laughter in their mouths. There is no better time to be in Honey Hollow, to be alive than December.

After an entire day of nonstop baking, Dutch and I head for home. There were six different holiday parties the Cutie Pie Bakery catered today. Lily helped me zip across town making all of the deliveries, which consisted of mostly iced sugar cookies, but there was a fair amount of double chocolate cookies, cranberry white chocolate cookies, braided peppermint candy cane cookies, molasses drops, German spice cookies, dark chocolate truffles, and rum balls—we can never forget the rum balls. The bakery smelled divine, and even now as Dutch and I make our way up the steps, I take in the thick scent of sugar and vanilla. It's better than any perfume on the planet.

A small yellow piece of paper sits taped to the door.

"Huh. What's this?" I pluck it off and read it.

Come over in five minutes. I would say turn around and head on over right now, but Pancake probably deserves his dinner.

Love, Noah

"Aww. Would you look at that?" I turn toward his cabin-like rental and give a hearty wave before heading inside and giving Pancake a double helping of his Fancy Beast cat food. Salmon delight, his favorite. I always figure when I've had a rough day both Pancake and I should be treated.

I steal a quick moment to freshen my hair and dab on a little lipstick. I consider perfume, but then think better of it. There's not a man on the planet who doesn't prefer the scent of a fresh baked cookie. And just like that, Dutch and I speed across the street before giving a gentle knock on Noah's door.

It swings open, and Noah greets me with a slow blooming, devilish smile. His frame is wide and daunting, and suddenly I have the urge to explore every menacing inch of it. The scent of his cologne envelops me first, and I note a roaring fire crackling behind him. It's perfectly romantic, and it only adds to the fact I'm exploding with lust for him.

"Why hello, you handsome man," I say as he reels me into a hearty embrace. "You look stunningly like my boyfriend, same vibrant green eyes, same chiseled features, that dark glossy hair I would love to run my fingers through all night long, and that facial scruff that just drives me wild. But since he's far too busy to spend any time with me at all, maybe you and I can have a little fun instead?"

His head pitches back, and he moans a dull laugh. "Fine." Those smiling eyes penetrate me deeply. "But if the rumors are true, he's got a gun. We'd better hurry."

"Not to worry. I'll shield you with my own naked body."

His head cocks to the side, eyes slit to nothing. "I like the naked part. I suggest we get to that right away."

"In a second. Is that pizza I smell? Does that mean Ivy is here? That is her homing beacon, isn't it?" I tease.

Noah's chest rumbles with a laugh before he presses a firm kiss to my lips. "That's our pizza."

"Ours? I like the sound of that. It almost makes us sound like a couple."

Noah sweeps me off my feet with a twirl and we're on the sofa before we know it, with me on his lap and a slice of pizza in each of our hands.

"Are you ready?" He takes an aggressive bite of his pizza, his hungry eyes never leaving mine. The sexual tension radiates off him like heat off a New York sidewalk in July.

A sharp breath fills my lungs. "This is you being spontaneous, isn't it?"

"I may not be able to pull off three hearty days, but I can give you one wild night." His voice is low and commanding while his fingers swirl circles over the back of my head and it feels amazing.

"Yes," I whisper. "I want anything you're willing to give me."

His thumb glides gently over my cheek. "I want to give you everything. The world." His brows bounce. "I want everything with you, Lottie. The house with a white picket fence, kids—lots of kids."

My mouth falls open. "Lots of kids? I love kids." My head

lands over his shoulder until I'm looking up at him from under my lashes. "How many are we talking? One, two dozen?"

He belts out a laugh. "I love kids, too. How ever many please you. How about that?" He brushes the hair from my forehead and hitches it behind my ear. "And I know that you are going to be one spectacular mother. You're a wonderful person, Lottie." There's a sadness in his eyes, and I can't quite put my finger on why.

"Hey?" I pull back a bit. "You're not upset over that office visit with Dr. Ferdinand, are you? The only reason I brought Everett was because I didn't think you'd approve." I wince when I say it because we've both determined that I don't give too much thought on whether or not he approves about anything, but I mean that in the very best, the very nicest way. I get why he's like that, and it has everything to do with my safety.

"No, I'm not upset." He blinks toward the fire before looking as if he wanted to shoot Everett. "I mean, I'm not thrilled. It's Everett." He shakes his head, his gaze still set at the fire as if it were a portal to the past. "He's not my favorite person. And I can guarantee he feels the same."

"He mentioned something about a girl a while back. One you borrowed and didn't give back."

He glances to the ceiling. "Not this again. See? This is the exact reason we will never get along. I think it's fair to say we agree to disagree. And for the record, I have apologized—maybe not loud enough for him to hear it. But it's nice to know he's got a real talent for nurturing a grudge. And I know that you appreciate him as a friend, but please believe me when I say he is particularly interested in you because it's his petty way of getting back at me. I'm sorry, Lot. I'm sorry you were inadvertently dragged into this."

A throaty laugh comes from me as I put down my pizza and scratch at the soft scruff over his cheeks. "I promise I am not concerned. And Everett and I are simply friends. He has never tried anything funny. There's absolutely zero evidence he's trying to steal me away from you because of some high school-issued revenge. I think he really may be over it."

"Not if he's bringing it up. And not if he's bringing it up with you. He's planting a seed, Lottie. Tearing down my character one subtle dig at a time."

My arms dive around his neck as I pull him in. "Well, it's not working. In fact, one might even say it's backfiring spectacularly." I giggle into a kiss.

Noah secures his hand over the back of my head and holds me there, our lips enjoying one achingly soft, slow peck after the other. He nibbles on my bottom lip before tugging at it softly with his teeth.

A deep moan comes from him. "I vote we move the party to a different location."

"I second that vote."

Noah has me in his arms again as he swoops me through the living room, and Dutch roars to life, barking and dancing around Noah's feet as if threatening to trip him. The barking gets louder, full speed and top volume as if someone placed a megaphone to his snout. My feet scissor through the air, and I do my best to get him to stop with a wag of my finger, but he only increases in velocity.

"Would you hush?" I whisper it so loud and fast it almost sounds like a sneeze.

Noah pauses a moment. "What's that?"

"Oh, nothing. I was just—my stomach was growling."

He backtracks a few steps. "Let's get that pizza in you. I'm a patient man." His dimples dig in adorably, and I can't help but bite down over my lip at the offer.

"No way. Get me to that bedroom, Noah Fox. I have naughty

intentions with you, and I plan on initiating them sooner than later."

"I'm willing to bet my intentions are a little naughtier than yours."

"We'll see about that."

Noah's bedroom is spacious and sparse, which seems reasonable since he's both a man and a minimalist. The furniture has that rustic, masculine appeal with each piece fashioned together with logs. The headboard itself is a series of dark wooden logs that run horizontal, and it feels homey and right in every single way.

Just as Noah is about to land me onto the mattress, Dutch bounds in, yelping and barking, sprawling his massive body over the circumference of the bed.

"No, no, no!" I cover my eyes as Noah deposits me gently, and I feel a strange rush as my body pushes through the furry phantasm who is insistent on not missing one exciting moment of my life.

Noah pulls back, his face heavy with concern. "You've changed your mind." His serious eyes meet with mine. He pushes out a slow breath of frustration. "How about I take you to dinner? I'm sorry that I'm moving so fast."

"What? *No!*" I pull him down over me and hold him there with all my might. "I wasn't talking to you. I was talking to—" I glance over at Dutch who looks to be happily chewing on Noah's shoe. "Myself." I give a little shrug. "It's just something I like to do."

"You said no." He gets up, his hands in the air as if it were a stickup.

"No, no! It's just something I like to say. See there? I did it again."

His chest pumps with the idea of a laugh.

"Yes! I want you, Noah Corbin Fox." I climb to my knees and pull him back over me. The weight of his body feels as if it's something I've craved all my life. My lips find his, and we're hitting our stride again. "I love you, Noah. I want this and everything else with you, too." My hands ride over his rock-solid chest as I do my best to undo the buttons on his dress shirt.

His eyes remain pinned on mine as he inches up my sweater, away from the lip of my jeans, and my bare skin becomes exposed to the cool air in the room. Noah and I are going for the slow reveal, the slow tease, and it feels as if it's been a long time coming. Every last part of me is already titillated beyond measure.

His mouth opens just as his phone rings in his back pocket, and he squints as if he regretted even knowing what a phone was. Noah falls to his elbow and fishes it out of his pocket before looking at the screen.

"And here we go." He picks up and tucks it to his ear. "Fairbanks," he mouths my way.

And there we go. Who knew Dutch and Ivy would team up to be a dynamic duo capable of preventing coitus in a single bound? I scowl over at the happy pooch, and he drops his head between his paws and whines.

I feel the same, buddy. Exactly the same.

Noah hangs up and stares at me for a moment.

"You don't need to say it. She needs you. The office needs you. All of Ashford County needs you back at your desk eating pizza with Ivy and her miles of long red hair." I sling my arm around his neck as he falls next to me. "I get it. And I don't mind. I love your career. I love that you get to do something that makes you happy."

"Nothing makes me happy like you do." He dots a kiss to my lips.

"So, what's on the agenda?" I ask as he bounces to his feet and pulls his gun off the dresser that I hadn't even noticed was simply sitting there. Terrifying, really.

Noah's chest expands as he looks my way. His lips twist as if he were uncertain if he should say a word. "There's a dent in Bella Carter's car. I can't say much more."

"Oh, the dent!" I sit up, suddenly animated in a whole other way. "That's right!"

"Wait—you know about this?"

"Yes. I mean, I didn't hear the crash. But I saw the dent in Ned Sweeny's minivan and his busted taillight. I guess I forgot to mention it."

"What do you mean you forgot to mention it?" Noah looks incensed—oh, all right, he looks downright ticked.

"I mean, we've been so busy. I hardly see you. I was waiting for a chance to get you alone. Everett and I—"

"You told Everett?" His brows dip with disappointment, but it's his tone that lets me know he's hurt. "Lottie, why would you keep these details to yourself? This could be vital information that could solve this case and, believe it or not, no one wants this case solved more than I do."

I raise my hand slightly. "I might be able to match your vigor."

Noah sags a moment, a slight look of defeat in his eyes. "Ned Sweeny?" He pulls on his jacket, his face distressed as if I had just told him it was Ned Sweeny's body I discovered next.

"Yeah. I didn't confront him about it, but I saw it the night of the tree lighting. Everett saw the damage the night of the murder, but he had no idea who the van belonged to. Did you know that Bella and Ned were—"

"Related by marriage." He blinks a dry smile. "I did know that, Lot."

"Oh, and he has this vast collection of those creepy wooden dolls just like the one in Dr. Ferdinand's office. Do you think they were arguing about the doll?"

"No, Lot." He helps me up as we head back toward the living

room. "They were arguing because they're having a messy breakup. Dr. Ferdinand and Ned have been having an affair."

"*What?*" I shriek so loud, Dutch gives a bark to go along with it. "But he's got a wife! A sick one at that."

"And that, unfortunately, is how an affair works." He pulls me into his strong, warm arms, and I never want him to let go. "It usually happens when one person doesn't feel fulfilled by their partner. They go off and find whatever it is they're missing in someone else." Grief pulls down his features, and it makes me wonder if he's thinking about his own wife—ex-wife. "I hope I never make you feel that way, Lot."

"No way. And I'm certainly never going to look to Everett for a single thing."

His brows knot up as his chest rumbles with a laugh, taking my own body along for the trembling laugh. "It's not you I'm worried about. He has a way of getting what he wants, when he wants."

"He didn't get that girl you stole from him."

His eyes widen as if there was a bullet coming at him, and I cringe.

"Sorry! Bad example. How about we have a do-over? Our night of spontaneity sort of went sideways."

"I'm in." He lands a kiss to my lips. "You're welcome to stay. I have no idea when I'll be back."

"I think I'll head home to Pancake. I have a three a.m. wake-up call. It's the busiest month of the year. But if you happen to be on Main Street tomorrow, please stop in. I'll have all of your favorites on standby."

Noah walks me across the street before jumping into his truck and taking off with a wave.

Noah and Ivy are just now getting around to investigating Bella and the carnage she inflicted with her car that night.

Bella's ballistic brother comes to mind. Maybe I'll check him out next. I'd hate to point the finger at someone with merely hearsay. He's probably just your run-of-the-mill overprotective big brother.

Or maybe he's prone to bouts of icicle wielding insanity?

Either way, I'm about to find out.

CHAPTER 13

"Oh. Ma. Gah," Keelie struts the words out low and sporadic. It's her verbal shorthand for all things fantastic. And clearly the sight before us has taken her breath away.

"Breathe," I hiss. "The last thing I need is to pluck you off the floor."

"This is a virtual buffet of the male species. Who has time to breathe? And, dear Lord, if I pass out, don't you dare pluck me off the floor. I want one of these muscle men to give me mouth-to-luscious-mouth."

"And maybe an STD. Did you ever think of that? No offense,

but these guys all look as if they need to discharge their excess testosterone on the regular—and I doubt they're doing it alone."

It turns out, the place to find Mason Carter is the Ashford Hard Body Gym, a place that Keelie and I found ourselves intimately acquainted with last month while we were questioning Jules King during Collette Jenner's murder investigation. But this is no Skin Swim. Mason works in the Bicep Belt, otherwise known as the weight room.

"That's him." The teenager giving us a tour points toward a real live human being covered with flesh and thick, cable-like cords that distend from his tree trunk of a neck. Keelie suggested we cut to the chase and ask for him by name, pointing out the fact that dozens of girls most likely request him by his formal moniker. "Anyway. Enjoy your day pass."

She takes off and it's just Keelie and me, and about five hundred hard bodies oiled to perfection. On second thought, that's probably just sweat dripping down their well-chiseled bodies.

Keelie sighs. "Oh, hon, I have no idea where to begin. It's like letting a kid loose in a candy store. So many yummy abs and just one mouth to gobble them all up with. About how many times do you think I could give out my number before it becomes a problem?"

"Well, it is Christmas. I say let the good times ring."

She takes off for the free weights, and soon enough there's a handsome stack of muscles assisting her in the endeavor.

I suppose this is the part where I should take a cue from my bestie. My feet meander over to where Mason encourages a couple of lanky boys to grunt it out while hoisting metal wheels the size of hubcaps over their heads.

"Excuse me!" I give a flicker of my fingers as he looks my way, and why do I get the feeling I've suddenly morphed into my mother? "Can you help a girl out? I'm not looking to turn into the Hulk. I just want a little definition."

"Sure thing, little lady." He gives a hearty wink and leads us to the back where a bevy of miniature weights in a rainbow of fruity colors sit in a neat pyramid. And for the life of me, I thought they were toys set out to occupy the junior set.

"Try these." He hands me a pair of hot pink vinyl covered glorified paperweights, and I'm more than glad about it. The last thing I want is sore arms while whipping out the three million gingerbread cookies I need to produce en mass before next week.

"Oh, this is perfect. I just need to get a little strength in me. You know? I live in Honey Hollow, and the last few months really have me on edge. We've just had another murder. A *murder*! Can you believe it?"

Veins erupt from his neck and under his eyes, popping to the surface of his plum-colored skin. A disconcerting sight, but, nonetheless, I can't seem to look away. After all, I was trying to get a visceral reaction from him—if indeed he was the killer. But honestly? The rash of murders we've had as of late could pop the vein of even the most innocent of them all.

"So I've heard." He grunts as he helps position my arms out and wide like wings. "Tanner Redwood." He gives a wistful shake of the head.

My heart thumps unnaturally when he says his name. "Did you know him?"

His eyes meet with mine for a brief second, and someone lets their weights drop near the back, breaking the awkward spell.

"Yeah, I knew the twerp. He was leading my sister on like some kind of a moron—and apparently, half of Ashford County."

"Oh, wow. I bet that drives you *berserk*." It was Bella who hand-fed me her brother. I may as well utilize her terminology.

"It's like you know me."

"Brothers. You're all the same. You know one, you know 'em all." Not really, but hey, it seems to be working. "So, I hear he was killed with an icicle to the neck. Do you think someone's older brother finally got their hands on Tanner?" As in you? For the love of all things good and my sex life, confess already. I'm about ready to go berserk myself the next time I see Noah in the wild. It's a cruel thing to tell my lady parts to brace themselves for a gentleman caller only to have a homicide block you off at the pass.

He balks at the thought. "With an *icicle*? That's something only a girl would use. In fact, the police caught the woman who did it."

"But they haven't made any arrests so far." Suddenly I'm fearing for my freedom. And, my goodness, what if he knows it was me hovering over Tanner's lifeless body with the murder weapon in my hand?

Something only a girl would use.

I glare at him a moment for this sexist remark. I'm sure plenty of men have committed murder by way of frozen water. It's brilliant, really. Theoretically, it could melt, and the murder weapon could vanish altogether. Although, Noah let me know they have this particular murder weapon safely tucked in the freezer. Not that it helps with forensics, but they didn't know what else to do with it.

"They're probably just putting together a case, gathering evidence." He scratches his chin, his stalwart frame posturing toward a group of girls who just walked in wearing less than a bathing suit. "To be honest, if it were me, I would have just beaten the snot out of the kid. It was on my list of things to do, but the killer got there first."

I let out an exasperated sigh. Mason does not sound guilty in the least. Unless he's an expert at covering it up. If I were trying to get away with murder, I might employ the same tactic.

"Personally"—he goes on—"I think death was letting him off a little too easy. After what he did to my sister. What he was doing to me—" His body tenses, and his eyes get a faraway look in them as he leaves the room emotionally for a moment. "I would have made Tanner Redwood suffer a whole lot longer than the three seconds it took for him to pass out at the sight of his own blood. He probably broke his neck when he hit the ground. I doubt a little puncture wound like that could have proven lethal." He straightens my arms again as I continue to flap like a bird in flight. "Someone missed something. There's no way that dude died of a stab wound."

Could he be right?

I shake my head at him. "But it must have hit an artery."

Mason winces. "I wasn't there, but I heard there was hardly any blood. Now you tell me if it hit an artery."

One of the girls calls him by name, and he excuses himself as he takes off with his enormous chest puffed out as if he wanted to impress her.

I was there. I did see the blood. Although Mason is right, there didn't appear to be much. But, then again, Tanner was dressed like Santa. With all that red fabric, he was swimming in a pool of crimson despite the fact he had a puncture wound. I'll have to ask Noah what the coroner's report says. Not that he'll be willing to share it with me. He's stubborn that way. And fiercely loyal to Ivy. Okay—so he's fiercely loyal to his career, but some days it feels more like the former.

I'm about to head for Keelie, who happens to be giggling up a storm while not one but two marble statues come to life are currently assisting her. One beefcake has his arms wrapped around her legs and the other around her arms. It looks as if Christmas came early for Keelie after all.

A familiar pixie-haired brunette zips by and heads down the corridor toward a sign marked *women's locker room* and I don't hesitate to follow.

It's her! Dr. Feel Good! I bet she needs to keep toned and

trimmed to seduce all her patients. I can't believe she's having an affair with a very married, very creepy might I add, Ned Sweeny. I bet they do it on that sofa in her office while Darjeeling and his lookalike ogle them with those creepy side-eyed gazes and those perverted open-mouthed smiles.

I speed my way right into the dressing room, snapping up a towel as I enter and quickly wrapping it over my shoulders, mopping my face with it, mimicking her every motion as I take a seat beside her on the bench.

"Dr. Ferdinand!" My voice booms cheery as I work to take off my shoe just the way she's doing now.

"Lolita!" She comes back at me with just as much enthusiasm. "How are you doing? With two capable studs at the ready, I'm surprised you have any use for a gym." She offers a congratulatory chortle, and I laugh right along with her. Little does she know that I haven't had all that much action from either of them. I have no idea what to do with one of them, let alone two together. For a moment, I envision the three of us tangled in a mass of flesh and am quick to blink the mouthwatering malfeasance away.

"Yes, well"—I clear my throat—"a girl has got to have her *me* time. You certainly get that, don't you?" I work off my right shoe, but she's already down to her bra and panties, and I hope to high heaven she's about to either pop on a muumuu or employ that towel next to her. Heaven knows I've seen enough flesh at the Ashford Hard Body Gym to last a lifetime.

"Oh, I do." She flicks her wrist as if it's a given before whipping off her bra, and my head drops down as I pretend to struggle with my sock. "In fact, I've cut back on my own suitors. I think I'll limit myself to two or three. Quality over quantity." Her underwear hits the floor, and she thankfully picks up the bath towel next to her. I lift my head, fully expecting to find her comfortably wrapped in the makeshift robe but, unfortunately, she's taken a cue from me and wrapped it around her shoulders.

Just great. But hey, if this therapist gig doesn't work out, she can always get a job at Bazingas. Just sayin'.

"Quality is quantity." I grimace through the disjointed statement. Honestly, there's nothing more distracting than having a pair of nipples staring right at you.

She laughs at my misnomer while pulling her towel out at the ends, her body on full display, and now all I want to do is run screaming.

"Lolita, you are a mighty lucky lady to have two handsome men. I don't think I've ever been envious of anyone before, but I'm certainly envious of you. Keep up the good work. It's quite impressive." She starts to take off, and I panic.

"That dummy in your office"—my hands flail a moment—"I was thinking of getting one for my mother for Christmas. She's obsessed. It really takes a particular kind of person to have an affinity for them." My lips smack as if I were about to be sick. A particular kind of person? Read *insane*.

"It sure does. The client who gifted it to me is also one of the suitors I felt the need to cut back on. But I think he mentioned they were passed down to him generationally. So I'm afraid I'm of little help."

Figures. Ned's entire family line is creepy.

"I see. Sorry about the breakup. Was it mutual?" I shrug as if a mutual parting might be a consolatory prize of sorts and, believe me, it would be. I've been through my fair share of messy breakups and received no prizes, unless of course you count the biggest prize of them all—my freedom.

"Heavens no. If he had his druthers, we'd be wed in the spring. But he's also quite content in his current arrangement. I'm afraid the relationship was *deadlocked*." Her eyes flit to the side when she says the quasi-morbid word.

"Can I ask you something, off topic?"

"Anything, shoot."

"The night Tanner Redwood died, did you notice anything suspicious?"

Her body goes rigid, and she looks at me as if I've just held out a pair of handcuffs and asked for her wrists.

"My sister's ex-boyfriend is a suspect." I scoff as I say it—but conveniently leave out the fact that my sister is, too. "Which is ridiculous because he wouldn't hurt a fly. And really? An icicle? If my sister's boyfriend were to take down Tanner, I'm sure things would have gotten a lot more physical than a frozen spear of water."

"I quite agree. Male aggression on that level is usually expressed through their fists."

"Men." I roll my eyes as if playing along, but I'm actually right there with her. "So, in your professional opinion, do you think that rules out a man altogether as a prime suspect?"

Her mouth opens and closes before she expels a sigh. "Would you look at the time? I'd best be heading to the shower. I have a home visit later tonight."

I bet you do. Someone is about to get their sexual appetite satiated in thirty minutes or less.

She bolts for the shower, inadvertently mooning me in the process, and I'm forced to look away.

Kelly Ferdinand all but said she didn't think a man stabbed Tanner with that icicle. But she sure was quiet when asked to admit that a man didn't do it. Maybe there's something I'm missing here.

Mason sure doesn't think Tanner died from that puncture wound. But Tanner was indeed wounded with the icicle.

Unless—oh my goodness, unless...

CHAPTER 14

"Two killers?" Everett shovels another bite of steak into his mouth and chews on both it and my theory.

"Think about it. I mean, how can we be sure he died of that neck wound?"

The low lighting in Honey Hollow's premier Italian restaurant, Mangia, gives Everett an otherworldly appeal. The small votive candle flickering between us contours his features until he's monstrously handsome. Everett ran into the bakery just before it closed and picked up a box full of Christmas cookies for the holiday party down at the courthouse tomorrow. He asked if

I wanted to grab a quick bite across the street and discuss the case, and of course I couldn't say no. And, believe you me, I know what Noah would be thinking about our little tête-à-tête. But I really do appreciate the fact Everett doesn't seem to mind me bending his ear over Tanner's murder investigation. In fact, I find it refreshing. I guess in a way he is giving me something that Noah isn't, and the realization makes me grieve a little. It's not Noah's fault he can't share details of this case.

Dutch—who I'm quickly discovering is the loyalist Golden Retriever on all the planet—lands his paw over my shoulder, over and over, until I give him a little scratch between the ears. If he had his way, I'd be scratching him twenty-four seven.

Everett lifts his wine glass my way. "Only the coroner knows for sure how Tanner died. Lemon, you're petting that dog again, aren't you?"

"He's irresistible. Believe me, you would be doing the same if you could see him. And how I wish the whole world could see him. He's a magnificent creature. So, how exactly do I go about speaking with the coroner?"

He shakes his head. "You'd have to be in tight for him to say anything to you. They don't share information to the public. Or you need to be a member of the victim's family to get information."

"I bet the coroner loves cookies."

"Lemon." Those cobalt blue eyes hood over.

"What?"

"No cookies. Bring it up to Noah. Focus on getting through the Christmas season. Have you decorated your tree yet?"

"Have you decorated yours?"

"Touché. But in my defense, the lights are enough, and it's a small holiday miracle it's up at all."

"Duly noted. I like my lights just fine for now as well. And if I didn't know better, I'd think you were changing the subject. I was wooed here with the prospect of discussing a certain homicide investigation. Don't tell me you're going soft and following in your stepbrother's footsteps. The next thing you'll be telling me is that you forbid me to continue with the investigation."

"First, I will never go soft on you." His lids hood a notch as if he were trying to seduce me. "And second, I will not follow in Noah Fox's footsteps in any capacity. Rest assured. Feel free to talk about the Redwood murder all you want." He leans in, that serious gaze pressed into mine. "But let it go as far as your lips. Lemon, you have put yourself in risky, life-threatening situations, and because of that, I can't be a cheerleader to you digging any deeper."

A thousand words want to stream from my infamous lips all at once, none of them good. "Everett, you're my partner in crime. What am I going to do without you?"

He takes an angry bite of his steak, his steely gaze still pinned to mine as he quickly washes it down with his port.

"So, you're saying despite my words of caution you're still willing to pursue this?"

"I happen to have an incredible thirst for justice. I believe we share that on some level."

His lips twitch with a smile. "That we do. And because I appreciate you in one piece"—he lifts his glass and offers me a toast—"you just got your partner in crime back. Might I suggest the next time we hit up Dr. Ferdinand's office we leave the dead weight at the door? I think she'd have us doing some pretty interesting things on that sofa of hers if Noah wasn't haunting the room with his presence."

"Yeah, and I bet that dummy would love to watch."

"You shouldn't call her names."

"Very funny."

He shifts in his seat until he's leaning over the table a bit. "You know what else is very funny? What I did for you this afternoon." He's right back to being stone-cold. He can't help it. It's a part of his charm.

"What pray tell did you do for me?"

He glances to my right as if he could see Dutch drooling away for a slice of my lasagna. "I met with people—*interesting* people, on your behalf." His head circles toward Dutch as if alluding to something.

I take in a quick breath. "Please tell me you didn't go see some medium or psychic. They're all charlatans, I tell you."

"Are you?"

"I'm neither a medium nor a psychic. I just have—amazing vision. Twenty-to eternity." It certainly doesn't sound good any way I spin it. "So, what did they say? Did they read your palm? Let me guess. They offered to give you a full body reading. Was she cute at least?"

"No and yes. I might have a whole new ex brewing thanks to you. But from what I gleaned, you might have a permanent poltergeist on your hands."

"Says the charlatan. And if she's right, I'm not sure I'd mind too much. But I imagine if this keeps up, I'll have an entire spiritual menagerie to contend with. That could prove disastrous to both my sanity and my love life."

"You have no love life."

"Thank you for pointing that out." I scowl over at him and don't mind one bit.

A pizza box lands at the lip of the table, and we look up to find Noah blinking a short-lived smile our way.

"Hey, Lottie." He nods to the space in the booth next to me as if asking permission.

"Please, yes!" I pull him down next to me with a hearty

embrace as Dutch quickly ambles next to Everett. I take in Noah's spiced cologne, and it feels like a salve after a long, tiresome day. "You smell amazing." I land my lips to his, and my stomach dips as if we were on a roller coaster.

"As do you." His smile fades as he narrows his gaze at Everett. "Evening."

Everett lifts his fork before digging back into his meal. "You're just in time. Lemon and I were discussing your love life."

"We were not," I'm quick to refute the idea.

"You're right." Everett points his fork my way. "We were discussing your lack of a love life."

Noah's chest thumps with a dull laugh, but he's not happy. And those death rays he's shooting his former stepbrother aren't too reassuring that this night won't end with a good old-fashioned fistfight—or another Honey Hollow homicide.

Noah and Everett stare one another down a disconcerting amount of time. Dutch looks to the two of them and barks as if trying to break their ocular stronghold on one another. He really does have my back.

Noah purses his lips. "Lottie and I are happy. I'd like to think I'm enough for her. She's doesn't need anything you might be peddling."

Everett leans in. "She needs more than you know. But the irony is that you don't even know why."

"*Everett.*" I pull his name out as if it were a threat, and it just might be. "You have no right to even hint." My blood boils at not only Everett's implication, but the one I just let slip out as well.

"Lottie?" Noah inches back, his eyes examining me in a whole new light. "Are you and Everett hiding something from me?"

My mouth opens, and I take in a gargantuan breath. It is my every nightmare for my supernatural gift to become public knowledge. My word, the reason I never told my mother, never told Keelie, is because I would never want to put them in a position where they were tempted to tell another soul. The only person I voluntarily told was Nell, Keelie's grandmother whom I regard as my own. And she's never judged me. She certainly never sat across from me at dinner and lorded her knowledge of it over my boyfriend's head.

Now it's me glowering at Everett. "You have crossed one serious line tonight." My voice shakes as tears blur my vision. "Excuse me," I say as I push Noah out of the booth first.

"Lemon"—Everett bounces to his feet as well and lands Dutch in a spinning tizzy—"I'm sorry. I didn't mean for it to come out that way."

"How did you mean it?"

Noah holds a hand out to Everett. "What's going on? What are the two of you talking about? Lottie, does this have something to do with the case?"

My lips part as I look into Noah's breathtaking lime green eyes. Here it is, the moment in which I choose to either lie to the man I love or tell the truth. My head screams *say yes, it has everything to do with the case and be done with it*. But my heart shouts *don't you dare*.

I go with another option entirely and glower over at Everett once again. "I hope you're happy," I pant as I try my best to reel in my newfound rage. "You've opened a can of worms that neither of us can ever shut." My voice raises an octave and heads turn this way. "I have to get out of here." I turn to leave, and Noah gently pulls me his way.

"What's happening? Lottie, I want to help you."

I glance to Dutch and those laser red eyes. "Neither of you can ever help me."

Noah brings Everett forward with a violent yank. "What is it that you're privy to and I'm not? It's about her, isn't it? The girl I supposedly stole from you. Lottie is nothing more than revenge

GINGERBREAD AND DEADLY DREAD

on your part. It all circles back to that night and the fact you had your ego blown to pieces by some girl over a decade ago."

"Some girl?" Everett muses. "I'm sure she'd love to know you've reduced her to less than a pronoun."

"Lottie is my girl—and you stay the hell away from her."

Everett slams his hands into Noah's chest and sends him stumbling into the table behind us, knocking glasses to their sides, customers bolting upright and screaming.

I don't stick around for the rest of the show. Instead, I run out the door and into the frozen December night with both Noah and Everett on my heels.

They call my name out as I head across the street to the Cutie Pie Bakery and Cakery. Yelling ensues as they argue amongst themselves.

"You stay here," Noah barks at Everett. "You don't get to do this."

Footfalls come in fast from behind, and before I can open the door to my van, Noah's hand lands gently over mine.

I turn and look into those heavenly eyes.

"You don't have to tell me, Lottie. Not unless you're ready. And if you're never ready"—he swallows hard as if already regretting what comes next—"then I guess I don't have to know."

I shake my head just enough. My hand rises to his prickly five o'clock shadow. "You said the right words, Noah. But it will eat you up inside, the not knowing."

"Lottie, I love you—in fact, you're the love of my life. But what could be so horrible that you wouldn't want to share it with me? I would never judge you."

"I know." I say a quick goodnight, jump into the van with my invisible dog, and take off.

Noah was right. Everett wedged his way between us, but not in the way Noah thought he would. I don't believe Everett meant to ruin things for Noah and me.

ADDISON MOORE

I can't blame Everett. I knew he was holding a live—or in my case a very undead grenade. I was the one who handed it to him.

It was only a matter of time before it went off.

I suppose the only way out of this mess is to tell Noah.

Dutch catches my eye, and I shake my head.

There's not a ghost of a chance.

CHAPTER 15

Somehow, last night, after that fiasco at Mangia and before I cried myself to sleep, I managed to convince Margo from the Honey Pot Diner to open the bakery for me—and bake a couple dozen breakfast goodies that I usually have hot and ready for the early crew of patrons. I apologized up and down and swore it would never happen again, but she was more than fine with it. She mentioned something about leaving for the holidays with her husband Mannon in a few days, and this would give her an opportunity to get some baking in for her family as well. Margo and Mannon are the Honey Pot Diner's five-star chefs that eschewed city life for our cozy small town.

Pancake and Dutch watch my every weary move as I caffeinate myself, shower, dress, put my face on, caffeinate myself again and again in hopes to get my bearings on a day that's started without me.

I'm just about to drain coffee number five when I spot a woman in a green jacket run up Everett's porch. Probably another ex. Hey? Maybe I'll be witness to a good old-fashioned egging? That would be fun. Maybe I can convince her to egg Noah's house, too? I'm sure he'll be my ex in no time. On second thought, maybe I can get her to throw a couple of eggs at me. Maybe that will be the cure I need to get me off the supernatural express.

Dutch whimpers as if he understood.

"You're the best," I say it sad and forlorn as I give him a scratch behind his ears. And I'm just about to do the same for Pancake when the woman in the green jacket bolts back down Everett's steps with a package in her arms. What's this? A delivery gone bad? Funny, she didn't come up with a package.

The package thief!

"Stop!" I roar as I bullet out of the house. "*Stop, thief!*" I scream at top volume.

The woman looks over, her eyes wide with surprise. That oversized package looks cumbersome in her arms. She glances around the vicinity until she spots a couple of taillights floating down the street, and she takes off in that direction.

"*Hey!*" I shout as Dutch bounds ahead of me in her direction. "Stop right there! This is a citizen's arrest!" But she's already halfway to her fickle getaway vehicle and my feet slow down as the sidewalk grows slick.

Dutch comes up on her and leaps right through her back. The woman jerks and seizes as if she felt the supernatural disturbance, and the package goes flying a good three feet above her head. But Dutch never hits the ground. He remains there, frozen midair, his entire body bursts into a brilliant flash of light before he detonates in a plume of smoke, evaporating to nothing.

"*Dutch!*" I cry out in grief. All of the pain, the agony that I'm embroiled in, roars out in that one vocal cord shredding burst. It's horrible enough to feel as if I've lost both Everett and Noah. Losing Dutch feels like the final blow.

A man in a dark suit rips past me and practically tackles the woman in the green jacket before she can make her escape. The getaway vehicle jerks a few times before peeling out of the neighborhood, the tires squealing in its wake.

"Lot!" He turns to me, and it's then I realize it's Noah. "Call 911!"

I speed back to the house and dial for help as fast as I can. No sooner do I put my coat on and head back out than the sheriffs close in, three cars strong, and the woman in the green coat is taken away as if she was never here.

The package lies on its side, abandoned on a neighbor's front lawn, and I snatch it up while Noah finishes up speaking with the deputy.

He jogs up alongside me. "Hey"—those soulful eyes penetrate me a moment before he lifts the package from my arms—"let me get that."

"I'll take it home. I won't be able to focus today if I know we left it outside just waiting for another thief to come along."

"Hopefully, that won't happen. And on a bright note, you may have just busted that package theft ring."

I can't help but shoot a wry smile to Noah. "The driver got away in the event you didn't notice."

"Silver Buick. Ninety-eight. My dad drove one. I got half the plate, so hopefully that will help. But you're right. In the meantime, we should remain vigilant." He hikes the package in the air a couple of inches.

We pause at the base of my porch, and that forlorn look in his gorgeous eyes says it all.

"Lottie, let me set it down." His dimples dig in, no smile, and he's got me in more ways than he could ever imagine.

I lead us up the stairs and into the living room. Noah sets the package on the coffee table and looks up slowly at the Douglas fir Everett helped me schlep inside as I seal the door shut behind us. No Dutch and it stings, but I'm hopeful he'll make another supernatural reprisal sooner than later.

"You got a tree." There's a marked sadness in his voice. "It's beautiful." Noah comes over, his arms landing around my waist just as Pancake lets out a rawrr of approval. Or disapproval, but personally, I like the former option. "Everett?" He ticks his head back toward the Christmas tree, that ever-growing sadness prominent in his eyes.

I give a quick nod.

"I'm just glad you have one." He swallows hard, making his Adam's apple rise and fall dramatically. "Lottie, I meant what I said last night. You are the love of my life, and if there's something you're not comfortable sharing with me, I'm okay with it. It has no bearings on my feelings for you—no bearings on us. But what I'm not okay with is letting it get between us. Everett let me know that whatever it was, you weren't enthused to share it with him. He said it was something shy of blackmail, the way he wrangled it from you. I'm sorry about that. But I'm not sorry that Everett is showing his true colors." His hands gently cup my face. "Last night was misery. It was a knife in my chest to know that I had upset you. Forgive me, Lottie. There's nothing more that I want than to move on."

My shoulders bounce. "Trust me, there's nothing to forgive. And it's me who feels terrible." I bite down hard over my lower lip in an effort to keep my emotions in check. "Did you mean what you said? The fact I have a secret has no bearings on us?" It almost hurts to look him in the eyes. The fact I have a secret from the love of my life is stifling. It's a horror, and I can't imagine how Noah and I will jump through this ring of fire and survive, but I'm hopeful.

His hands warm my back as he presses me closer. "No bearings whatsoever, I promise. It won't be mentioned again." He drops a kiss over the top of my head before pulling back to get a better look at me. "Did I hear you call out *dutch* out there?"

My mouth opens as if something useful were actually about to come out, and his brows knot with concern before smoothing over.

"This wouldn't happen to have anything to do with that which won't be mentioned, does it?"

"I—uh…" A guilty shrug rises and falls on my shoulders.

"Then it's not necessary." His gaze softens as he takes me in. "You're beautiful and you're sweet and kind. You are everything I've ever wanted. I just need to know you're mine."

"I'm yours." I don't hesitate with the words. "All of me, even the unspoken parts. They all belong to you, Noah."

His chest expands right along with his lips. They land on mine, and he takes my mouth. Noah pours his heart, his soul, his every *I'm sorry* into that one luscious exchange. It says *wait for me. Be patient, our time will come. Here is a taste of what I have to offer.*

A soft moan works its way up my throat as I leash my arms around his neck. Sometimes you know something to be beautifully true, and Noah and I are that truth. Innately, we are simply right and meant to be.

This man right here has been my destiny all along.

This much I know is true.

Now, if only we can catch that killer and exchange the best gifts of all this holiday season—each other.

CHAPTER 16

Honey Hollow is beautiful year-round, but the splendor of the holidays only seems to highlight its beauty. And because of that beauty, the Lemon family is rife with traditions. In the spring, we picnic in the countryside. In the summer, we spend endless lazy days by Honey Lake. Fall brings a riot of color in all of the surrounding trees, and we bask in the rich bounty from the earth. Winter, well, winter reigns supreme as she ices the housetops with glittering snow, but it's the yearly trip to look at the holiday lights with my sisters that I look forward to the most.

Lainey holds the screen of her phone out the window as we

travel through neighborhood after neighborhood sharing the magic of the lighted holiday displays with our sister Meg. Meg is one year younger than me, and miles stronger as evidenced by her successful run on the Vegas female wrestling circuit. Her onstage, or should I say in ring persona is called Madge the Badge, complete with jet-black dyed hair down to her rear, and haunting yellow contacts, which I've only recently noticed have a line running vertically down the iris like that of a cat. Meg is a riot, good-natured, and a lot of fun to have around in general, so I don't mind the fact that I'll be adding a new leg to our adventure tonight. In fact, I think she'll rather enjoy it.

"Farmington Way?" Lainey shoots me a look before getting back to the task of holding the phone out the window. It's a balmy thirty degrees out, and even though I assured Lainey it would be fine to roll up the window, she insisted on nothing but an unobstructed view for our saucy little sis. "Hey, turn this train around. There's only one more house coming up, and it's dark. This is getting depressing."

"The holiday light tour is over. We're starting a new tour," I say as I park just shy of the driveway.

"What kind of tour?" Lainey sounds as if she'd rather alphabetize every book in the entire library all over again rather than go along with anything I have planned.

"Relax," I say, unclicking my seat belt. "It's just a quick stop. Ned Sweeny invited me up to see his vast and impressive wooden doll collection."

Meg breaks out into a hyena-like laugh. "Holy smokes!" She digs her pinkies into her eyes to stop the spontaneous flood of tears. "Some guy asked you to his place to see his woody, and you bring your sister along for the ride? I'm betting those boyfriends of yours don't know about this dude. Who would have thought little Lot would be gunning for a dating roster? If you get seven, you can rotate one each night."

Lainey scoffs. "Stick with six. Take a night off, sister."

"I only have one boyfriend," I'm quick to correct. "Not plural. Just the one and his name is Noah."

Meg leans into the camera. "Have you seen his woody?"

"Would you"—I bat the phone away—"No, but I will. And that's none of your business, by the way."

Meg grunts, "Mom says you've got two of 'em. She says you're juggling a detective *and* a judge. Way to cover your bases if you ever get busted for a felony."

I avert my eyes at the thought, but hey, she's got a point.

"Come on." I nudge Lainey to get out, and she begrudgingly follows me up the walkway to the Sweenys' enormous home. It has a medieval appeal, all dark wood and wrought iron, stone siding with ivy climbing up to the second level. As far as holiday displays go, it has nothing but a simple string of clear lights running along the lower level. The north end of Honey Hollow is definitely the ritzier side of town. The only person I know that lives out here is Mom's friend, Eve Hollister.

We come up on the beveled glass entry, and I ring the door-bell and wait several minutes but nothing. I ring and knock and give a polite *yoo-hoo* before Lainey pulls me away.

"Take a hint. They're either not home or wish we would go away," she hisses because she clearly wishes we would go away, too.

Meg tee-hees from the other end of the phone, and I take a moment to scowl at both of them.

"Go on, Lottie"—Meg whispers as if she needed to—"why don't you bust the door down? What's a little breaking and entering to a girl like you? I bet you've got the entire Ashford County Sheriff's Department in your back pocket. And if they show up, simply tell 'em you got a personal invite to see Mr. Sweeny's woody." She bursts out with the choo-choo train laugh she used to employ while shooting soda out of her nose when we were kids. Like I said, Meg has always been a real riot. Note, I am not laughing.

"I'm not busting down the door," I say as I back up and inspect the mega mansion. Save for the porch light, the rest of the house is dark. It's clear no one is home. Or to Lainey's point, faking it.

Hey? Didn't Ned mention that his study was downstairs? A four-car garage eats up the left side of the house with a simple pine wreath over each door.

"It must be this way," I whisper as I lead us to the right.

"What must be this way?" Lainey gasps. "Lottie, we're trespassing on someone else's property. They shoot people for less than this!"

"Nobody is going to shoot you," I hiss as I make my way to the corner of the enormous structure. A large window sits curtainless, exposing a dark cave beyond our visual reach, so I do the only thing I can think of. I turn on the flashlight to my phone and shine it inside.

"Oh my stars!" Lainey barks unexpectedly. "What the heck are you doing? People are going to think we're thieves!"

"We're not thieves." I make my way around to the side of the house, and I can hear Meg giggling herself into a conniption.

"Breaking and entering!" Meg cackles. "Knew it!" It sounds as if she's slapping her knee.

Lainey growls at the phone. "Oh, hush. You do realize that if we're caught, you'll be an accessory to a crime."

"Lottie Kenzie Lemon!" Meg's voice riots into the night. "Get off that man's property and go find that boyfriend of yours to show you his vast and impressive woody!"

And on that note, Lainey clicks off the phone.

The side window is at just the right height for me to reach for it on my tiptoes, and as I glide my fingers over the glass, sure enough, it moves. I wince a little after the fact because I just realized I left my fingerprints all over them like a calling card.

"It's open," I whisper. "I'm going to need a boost."

"*What?* Are you insane? I'm not giving you a boost."

"You want to go home, don't you? Besides, I'm not insane. I'm not going inside. I'm just going to poke my head into the window, and we'll be out of here in no time."

"Oh My WORD. The things I do for you. I sure hope you have a Cadillac waiting for me under the tree come Christmas morning." She threads her fingers together, and I step over her palm like the wobbly step it's proving to be.

"Would you hold still?" My voice warbles as I do my best to get the window to budge and, sure enough, it opens with a yawn. The harsh smell of mothballs and that pine-scented wood cleaner my mother douses the B&B with clots up my nostrils. This must be the right place. I shimmy up onto my elbows and poke my upper torso inside. It takes a coordinated effort to shine my light into the cavernous space and—

A strangled scream gets locked in my throat as a million smiling faces stare back at me. The whites of their unnaturally large eyes glisten like warning beacons, and a gripping fear seizes me, causing me to lose my balance and nosedive inside.

"Oh my word!" I hiss as I hit the floor in a crumpled mass of limbs. "Oh geez." My heart palpitates violent and strong like an elephant stampede—if that poor herd of elephants was subjected to a vast and unimpressive wooden dummy collection. This right here is B-rated horror movie action that I never wanted to be a part of.

Holy mother of all things good and evil.

I shine the light back onto the bevy of faces, and note that they're all secured to the wall somehow. At least twenty across and fifteen high along the vaulted ceiling. A large pine desk sits in the center of the room, and I scramble to my feet and head over on pure adrenaline. All of these nonliving eyes feasted on me have me terrified, have my entire body beating along with my petrified heart. I sweep my flashlight over the desk. Nothing but a few books on ventriloquism, a book on indoor winter gardens, and a mug full of pens. I pull my sleeve over my fingers and glide the desk drawer open, and it lets out an egregious squeak. Even though it's probably too late to cloak my fingerprints, it doesn't hurt trying.

A few more pens stare back at me, an entire litany of paperclips tangled in the wild. I tap my fingers further inside and come upon a magazine clipping, and I pull it forward. I cast the light over it and gasp. It's a picture of Ned and Dr. Ferdinand. They're both dressed in formalwear, and there are plenty of other people in the background. The caption beneath them reads *The Garland Gala's guests show some flare!*

"Huh." The Garland Gala is a fancy charity ball they hold in Ashford every year. I pull the magazine closer to get a better look. There's a man in the background, arms folded over an enormous chest, that scowl on his bearded face. He looks familiar. I've seen him somewhere, but I can't quite place him.

Slowly, I slide open the three side drawers. Nothing but a bunch of clippings and magazines on the wooden creatures that are prone to kill him in his sleep. I shine the light to the small trash can near the desk, and I can hear Lainey hissing something my way. I unravel a few pieces of paper and nothing. I reach down and fish out the final one lingering against the liner as if it didn't want me to touch it. I open it up and shudder. It's an invitation to the Parks and Rec holiday celebration. There's a splashy picture of a cartoon Santa surrounded by a bevy of sexy female elves. That sounds about right. Underneath the cartoon it reads *Starring our very own Tanner Redwood as Santa!* Tanner's name is underlined in pencil.

Huh. I turn the page over to the roster of the other acts and scan down the list, surprised to see that Ned Sweeny's name is nowhere to be found. But I was there. He had Darjeeling. He said they were going to go on, right? Why would he lie about that? Maybe he was added last minute. Maybe that's why he underlined Tanner's name, so he knew who to contact.

I shine my light to those stony faces staring at me on the wall and make my way over. My entire body thumps as if my soul were begging to be evicted. There's a clothing rack to the right, a row of suits, and I pluck at a few of them before coming to the checkered one Ned was wearing the night of the murder.

"Lottie!" my sister squeals just as headlights pull into the driveway, and I nosedive my way right back out and into the holly bushes to the left of the window in hopes of a soft landing. Sorry to say, not so much.

A pair of footsteps head over at a quickened pace, landing both Lainey and me into a spastic tizzy. For a moment, I use my sister as a human shield until I remember that I'm the one that dragged her into this mess, and thus it's me who actually deserves to die—so I reverse our places, my arms outstretched behind me in an effort to cage her in.

"*Freeze*," a man's voice gruffs into the night as he takes a defiant stance, the moon shining down on a black gun pointed in our direction.

"Dear Lord up in heaven, don't shoot!" I squeeze my eyes shut tight and prepare for the worst.

"Lottie?" That deep, warm voice sounds far too familiar and I pry an eye open, hoping I'm both wrong and right.

"Noah?"

"Geez." He tucks his weapon into his back and speeds over. "There's a call out for a security system breach."

"I can explain everything. It's a total misunderstanding," I belt the words out so fast it sounds like gibberish.

"Listen to me. I'm only going to say this once." His face elongates in the shadows, and his stern eyes press into mine with an unspoken threat. "Get in your car and leave now. You have exactly one minute and thirty seconds before a squad car shows up and—"

He doesn't finish his sentence before Lainey and I are back in my hatchback and halfway down the road.

Lainey smacks me on the arm. "I'm never getting into a car with you ever again. I don't even care if you're behind the wheel!"

"So, does this mean we won't be driving to the Evergreen Manor together tomorrow night for the annual Honey Hollow Christmas party?"

"You'll be lucky if you're not spending tomorrow night in a jail cell! You crossed one serious line tonight, missy."

"All right. I did. I'm sorry. I just got a little carried away. It was Meg's fault for seeding the idea into my brain to begin with." That's always been my go-to—when the going gets rough, blame Meg.

"It's not Meg's fault, and you know it. You're obsessed with finding these murderers. It's all you think about!"

"Because I am trying to clear your name and your boyfriend's! Who, by the way, has a very flimsy alibi. You both do." I gasp as I pull onto my sister's street. "Say, the two of you didn't actually off Tanner, did you?" I stop the car in front of her house, and Lainey swings the door open, letting the icy wind have its way with us once again.

"No! Of course not." She gets out and ducks back in for a moment. "And look, I do appreciate you going out on a limb for us, but you have to understand that we don't want you ending up with a rap sheet over it." Her eyes squint to nothing. "Wait a minute. You've been complaining nonstop over the fact you and Noah haven't had your penciled in sexy date night yet. This isn't about Forest and me at all, is it?" Her mouth falls open with the revelation. "This is about Noah's woody!"

"*Out.*" I do my best to shoo her away. "Shut the door, Lainey, and goodnight. Let's pretend this never happened."

"Fine." She takes a meager step back. "So, did you learn anything new? See any decent clues that can take you one step closer to a mattress?"

I think on it for a moment. "I already knew he was having an affair with Dr. Ferdinand."

Lainey makes a face. "You mean, she was sleeping with both Tanner and Ned Sweeny? That's quite a range. I guess that woman would sleep with anyone and his brother."

Brother. Brother? It's as if a light goes off.

"That man with the beard! It was Bella's brother—Mason Carter." A laugh stifles in my throat. "He was giving Ned Sweeny a look as if he wanted to kill him for having his arm around Dr. Ferdinand."

"I have no clue what you're talking about, but my uneducated guess is that the man with the beard was sleeping with her, too. What does any of this have to do with solving Tanner's murder?"

"Everything and maybe nothing." I shrug. "Sorry about the breaking and entering." I'd say it wouldn't happen again, but at this point in my life I can't guarantee it.

"No problem." She waves it off. "Meg is right. You've got the entire judicial system in your back pocket. Sure doesn't hurt to have boyfriends in high places." She shuts the door and takes off with a wave of her fingers.

I roll down the window and pull up a bit. "Boyfriend!" I shout over at her. "*Singular!*"

Noah comes to mind, and a devilish smile glides over my face.

That man should have arrested me, and he let me go.

He loves me after all.

CHAPTER 17

*U*sually on a frosty night like tonight, there's nothing better than curling up with a good book, a cup of hot cocoa, and my cat, Pancake, by a roaring fire. But tonight is no usual night.

After dropping Lainey off at her place and listening to her salty reprimands regarding that little breaking and entering faux pas, I've lost my ability to focus on reading a book. My cocoa is far too hot to enjoy, and both Pancake and I miss Dutch far too much for it to ever be reasonable. Not to mention the fact I can't stand it when Lainey is upset with me. I tried to point out that I came by the break-in honestly. It was never my intent to encase myself in a room with a hundred haunted faces staring back at me. The breeze picked up, and I fell inside. And, honestly, there was no theft, no damage to the property as all of those wooden eyes that were feasted upon me can attest—and most importantly, we weren't hauled down to the Ashford Sheriff's Department and booked. And to her salty rebukes, I responded with the only way I knew how—all is well that ends well and every other maxim that is on my side.

No sooner do I stoke the fire than a gentle knock erupts at the door.

"Who could that be?" I ask, swooping up Pancake into my arms. I don't know why I do it, but I've trained myself not to open a door without him when there's a potential stranger on the other side. I think deep down inside I like the thought of Pancake providing a first line of defense in the event I'm attacked. Not that I would open the door to just anyone. I peer through the living room window and spot an all too familiar frame on the porch holding a couple of boxes of pizza.

I swing open the door, and Noah offers a defeated short-lived grin. "Pizza delivery."

"How did you guess I was hungry?" I can't help but bite down on my lip as I let him inside.

"Because I happened to see you work up an appetite." His brows twitch as I take the pizzas from him and he removes his jacket. "You mind if I steal a slice?"

"You can steal a whole pie. You do realize you bought two, right? Is one for Ivy?"

"Funny." He pulls me into his arms. "I'm off for tonight. I thought maybe since we can't seem to make headway on our alone time that we might be able to put our great minds together and try to remove the obstacle that's keeping us apart."

"The *case*?" I inch back and examine him. "Are you, Noah

Corbin Fox, inviting me, Lottie Kenzie Lemon, into your investigation?"

His lips twitch as if unsure of what direction to go in. "Not exactly. The detective in me that is on probation down at the Ashford's Sheriff's Department still very much does not want you in any way to jeopardize those nice paychecks he's quickly getting used to." He tilts his head to the side, and there's an adorable boyishness about him right now. "But every other part of me is overriding that fool because I want nothing more than some serious alone time with my girlfriend." His finger caresses my jawline. "I had an idea earlier. We both spill everything we know, no-holds-barred."

"A wrestling term. Now that's something I can relate to on a sibling level. What about Ivy?"

"She will never know. I can lose my job over this."

"Then you must really trust me."

"With my life."

A breath hitches in my throat. "It sounds like you're calling a momentary cease-fire."

"Accepted?"

"Yes, now let's get to solving this case."

Noah and I land on the rug in front of the fireplace, noshing on pizza, washing it down with the few measly water bottles I had rolling around in the fridge, and talking about everything under the sun besides that aforementioned obstacle. The sparkling white twinkle lights on the Christmas tree add an aura of magic to the room, and the fire ensures that a romantic time will be had by all. Tanner Redwood flashes through my mind as if refuting the theory, and I have always hated it when Tanner is right.

"You know"—I toss my crust back on the coffee table and scoot in close to him—"you never did tell me much about your family. I think you mentioned a brother, Alex?"

"Yup. A Marine turned investment banker. He's doing well for himself in Fallbrook. My mother moved to Florida a few years back, but we were never close. After my dad and she went their separate ways, my mom floated in and out of relationships. They were so bad my dad had us boys move in with him."

"What about Christmas?" I give a cautious shrug. Noah spent Thanksgiving here with my family and me, so did Everett, but I would think Christmas might be different.

"Alex and his girlfriend will be with her family. I'm sure we'll enjoy a rather nice phone call that lasts less than five minutes. Same with my mother." There's a touch of grief in his eyes as if he wished it wasn't so.

"You'll be with my family and me at the B&B and I won't take no for an answer."

He glides me over his knees until I'm seated on his lap.

"That's very nice of you, Lottie. Invitation accepted. If you're there, then that's where I want to be."

My insides melt at his kind words. "You're my family, Noah. I mean it."

"In that case, I'd like to make dinner for you after the holiday. Just you and me at my place as a way to say thank you. If you don't mind, I'll relegate dessert in your capable hands."

"Aye aye, sir. I'm good at following orders."

His brows pinch, amused. "I'll remember that."

His lips land over mine slowly and methodical, the kind of kiss you give when you know you don't have anywhere to go for hours and you can take your time doing just this.

Noah pulls away slowly, his lids still hooded thick with lust.

"Is that a taste of things to come?" I give that scruff on his cheeks that I love so much a quick scratch. Noah's warm cologne casts its spell on me the moment he walked through the door.

"Exactly." A dark rumble of a laugh pumps through him. "Now let's get down to business so—"

"So we can get down to business." I spin around to face him fully. "First suspect."

"Forest Donovan."

"Forest is innocent, and we both know it."

Noah winces. "He's got a great motive, and he argued with the deceased just moments before you discovered his body. Ivy and I shook the poor guy down. He even volunteered for a polygraph."

"Well, there you go. I mean, someone who is guilty wouldn't volunteer to have their innocence legally questioned."

"That's the thing. A polygraph isn't admissible in court. You may as well introduce psychics or pull out the tarot cards. It doesn't mean a whole lot. And he might know just enough about the law to realize that."

I shake my head. "Next?"

"Your sister, Lainey."

"She didn't kill him, but she should have. And before you get to the prime suspect, yours truly, I should have killed him, too."

"Who's your top suspect, Lottie?" His fingers dig into the back of my hair, and I'm about to say to hell with the homicide investigation, let's open a whole new investigation—with each other.

"I don't know. It's a draw. There's Bella Carter—the Bazingas' waitress. She was having a fling with him, and things went sour. I saw him wearing her like an accessory just before the party got underway that infamous night. Then there's Kelly Ferdinand, our favorite sex therapist."

His dimples cinch in. His lids hood dangerously low. "Whose services we won't be needing—I assure you of that."

A dirty laugh gurgles in my throat. "Kelly attached herself to him like a barnacle when my sister caught them. It was a sizzling blur of emotions. I don't know where Kelly took off to, but Tanner took off not long after. Kelly could have done it. She said some creepy things about her younger suitor when I met up with her at the gym."

"You met up with Kelly at the gym?" His head ticks back a notch, and I can't tell if he's impressed or not.

"I suppose that's below Ivy's investigative standards. But that also happens to be where I met up with Mason Carter, Bella's brother. It turns out, Mason wasn't so happy that Bella had her heart broken. Maybe he did go berserk and kill him? Then there's Ned Sweeny and all those strange wooden dummies. I still can't figure out how he factors into this, but let's face it, those wooden toys he plays with puts him on the suspect list whether he likes it or not. Plus, he was having an affair with Kelly. Maybe Tanner knew something? Maybe he was threatening to tell Ned's wife?"

Noah takes an enormous breath as he looks to the ceiling. "Maybe. Have you checked out Tanner's siblings?"

"Rachel is pregnant with her first child. Hook is busy with the family business. I don't think either is responsible."

Noah's brows bounce. "You don't think one of them offed Tanner? Rachel could be bitter that she was left out of the real estate business."

"Maybe so, but she still collects a check from it."

Noah gives a hard blink toward the fire. "The father only wanted his sons to run the business. Chauvinistic much? And now that Tanner is out of the picture, Hook is in charge."

"I guess we need to talk to Hook again."

"I did." He shakes his head. "He actually seemed bitter he needed to give up life in the city but said he was taking one for the Redwood team. It doesn't seem like a life he would have chosen, let alone killed for. It's a great cover though if he did it."

I make a note to speak with Hook again.

Noah nods my way. "What about Chrissy Nash?"

"The mayor's ex-wife? What about her?" She and my mother have been friends for years. Chrissy is in on all of my mother's shenanigans, including every book and travel club under the Honey Hollow sun.

"They were having an affair."

"*What?*" I squawk so loud Pancake rawrrs right at us, and I'm suddenly fearing for Noah's eyes.

"You mean the infallible Lottie Lemon was not privy to this information?" His chest rumbles with a laugh. "I'm questioning the validity of the claim."

"Who made it?"

"Chrissy confessed to Ivy. She thought she might come under the spotlight. And I know I don't need to ask, but please don't say a word."

"I wouldn't dare. Wow, Tanner really was sleeping with half the town. I can't see Chrissy doing anything like this. But then, everyone's motives seem rather weak." A thought comes to me. "You know, while I was in Ned's study, I saw this picture. It was Ned and Kelly at some function last year, and in the background there was this man—he looked familiar, but I couldn't quite place him. But it occurred to me a little while ago that it was Mason Carter. He seemed to be glaring at the two of them. It was creepy. Oh, and Ned had a flyer for the holiday party, but his name wasn't on the roster of performers. I could have sworn he said he was going up on stage with Darjeeling."

"Darjeeling?" His brows hike a notch. "It's nice to see you're on a first-name basis with Ned's—"

"Don't you dare call him his woody." Meg and that seedy conversation come to mind.

"Whoa." Noah lifts his hands a moment. "This just took a turn."

"Let's get back on track. I don't think I can stand the fact I'm sitting on your lap and talking about someone else's woody. What about Tim Wagner?"

"The kid with the chip on his shoulder? I don't know. Sure, he seemed angry, but he has another job. A new girlfriend. A lot to lose. And to be honest, I just don't see a guy offing Tanner that way."

"So you think the murderer is a woman. How very sexist of you." I bite down a smile.

"Sorry," he mouths the word. "What do you think?"

"I think it was a woman. And I think it could have been a man, too. Mason Carter suggested that maybe the icicle didn't kill him, that maybe it was a flesh wound. It got me thinking, maybe there were two killers."

Noah glances to the fire. You can practically see his wheels churning at a million miles an hour. "There was no other outward sign of trauma."

"Collette Jenner died of poisoning. There were no outward signs of trauma."

He shakes his head. "Can't be."

"Maybe he was strangled after the fact?"

He moans as if disagreeing. "Considering he had a neck wound, that would have been messy."

"Can't you have them check the body once again?"

"The one we buried last week?"

"Yes, that one. They exhume bodies all the time on TV."

"And the network foots the bill because it's fiction." Noah closes his eyes a moment. "I think I need to get back to my desk and check out the coroner's report one more time. I'll go over the case file and see if anything rings a bell now that we've gone over it in detail."

He helps me to my feet, and I dive a heated kiss over his lips. "I hate that you have to leave. Do you know how hard it is to have your cookies left unfrosted?"

A warm laugh bucks from him. "Do you know how painfully uncomfortable a cold shower is in the middle of December? If it makes you feel better, I share your misery."

"If you do end up unearthing Tanner, let me know and I'll

show up to clobber him for getting himself killed just in time to ruin my fun." I wince. "That was terrible of me. Pretend you didn't hear it."

"I think Tanner would prefer a clobbering from you to someone else's slaughtering." He dips his lips to mine and lingers. "I'll let you know what I find out."

"Fine. See you at the Evergreen Manor tomorrow night for the annual Honey Hollow Christmas party?"

"You bet. I wouldn't miss it. And who knows?" he says, swinging his jacket back on. "Maybe the killer will be there, too."

"I'll pass on the side of homicide, thank you."

Noah pulls me in, his body warming mine, that look of longing still in his eyes. "I'm hungry for another meal altogether myself."

"Solve this case, Fox. I've got more to offer than a couple of cookies."

He winces. "That shower just got a heck of a lot colder."

"I'll join you when you get home, and we can roll around in the snow together."

I walk him out, and he points to the night sky, navy velvet with crushed diamonds glistening above.

"There are a lot of stars out tonight. Maybe make a couple dozen wishes."

We say a quick goodnight, and I watch as he takes off for Ashford.

I glare up at the sky a moment. "Come on, Tanner," I whisper into the frozen night. "Tell me who killed you. It's time to put both you and this case to rest." There's a holiday to be had—*and* a boyfriend to feast on.

A tiny spear of red light comes from down the street, past Everett's house, like twin taillights traveling in reverse. Only they're too small to be taillights. They look more like—

"Eyes!" I hop up and down as Dutch bounds his way back to

me, up my walkway, up my porch, and right into my arms, feeling every bit solid and real. "I missed you!" I kiss his fuzzy forehead as he tries his hardest to lick up a storm. "Don't you dare do that to me ever again. The least you can do is say goodbye."

We head in and he hurdles his way to Pancake, and they're both fast asleep before the fire goes out.

It's just me awake with no boyfriend to warm me, and no prime suspect to put an end to this misery. All night I ruminate on the things Noah and I talked about. There are so many moving parts to this case. So many viable suspects. Maybe he should arrest them all and be done with it. In the least put them in a holding cell for three days straight so Noah and I can get the edge off.

But that's not the way it goes. The truth is, one cold-blooded killer equals one too many cold showers and lonely nights.

I've never wanted to solve a case so bad.

I'm going to find that murderer, and then I'm going to kill them myself.

And just like that, I fall asleep with a smile on my face.

CHAPTER 18

The Evergreen Manor is decorated to the hilt with live garland trimming every inch around the room, hanging from every doorframe, and lying over the marble counters of the reception area. A sign posted at the entry of the main hall reads *Welcome to the Evergreen Manor Annual Honey Hollow Christmas Party and Tree Auction! Every penny earned from the auction goes directly to the Children's Hospital. Bid generously and win a beautifully decorated tree!*

Dutch dances a jig by my side as if he were happy to be here, and I'm sure in his present state, he's happy to be anywhere.

"Well, buddy, let's do this thing."

The Evergreen Manor itself is a beautiful inn. It's no wonder this is a tourist favorite among those who visit Honey Hollow. Mom's B&B gets the overflow, and with that she's plenty busy. But as beautiful as the garland is, and that magical pine scent it expels like the finest perfume, as adorable as the wreaths are, dotted with their cherry red bows, this place still gives me the shivers after poor Collette bit the big one right here not more than a month ago. It was all because Patricia Rutherford wanted her husband dead and buried. But he's neither of those things. In fact, he's very much alive and grinding his hips into my mother as they dance side by side.

The music pumping from the speakers is a touch too loud. Most likely because the maintenance manager at the Evergreen is playing Christmas carols from off his phone. Mutton O'Grady has been known to play DJ on more than one occasion.

"What are they doing?" Lainey hisses into my ear as we scowl at my mother and her newfound beau.

"Enjoying themselves?" It makes my stomach churn to think just how they might be doing so when in the confines of a secluded space. I know for a fact Mr. Rutherford has a penchant for all things kinky. Come to think of it, I'd better look into getting my mother a stun gun for Christmas to go along with that ring of my father's. I haven't told Lainey about it—the ring, not the stun gun. It's just as much a surprise for her as it is our mother. If only Noah were here, I might just forget all about Mr. Rutherford for the night. But Ivy insisted he work late.

I bet she did. She just loves having my Noah all to herself.

Lainey swats me. "Hey, have you checked out the trees for auction yet? They're so *cute*!" she trills those last few words out. "There's one with all these beautiful feathered masks dripping from it like jewels. I've already placed a bid on that one. Oh, and there's another one with nothing but baking goodies all over it. It's totally to die for. I bid on that one too just in case you didn't get around to it, but you should totally go ahead and outbid me. Lord knows I can't afford to win two trees tonight."

"I have a tree. But I suppose if it's for charity. Hey, maybe I can win it for Noah? Looking at all those baking baubles might actually remind him of me."

"Ha. You're a riot." She makes a face. "Still no cookies, huh?"

"It's the frosting I'm missing." I may have shared my quasi-raunchy convo with my sweet sis.

Forest comes up and wraps his arms around Lainey from behind before I can answer, and I can't help but think how intimate it looks. Lainey and Forest seem to have picked up right where they left off.

"Hey, Lottie," he says while twirling my sister in toward him. "How are things with you?"

"Just keeping busy with the bakery." And the latest fantastic phantasm I've seemed to attract. I glance over at Dutch who's running circles through the crowd on the dance floor. "In fact, I catered all the desserts here tonight."

"That's why they're so delicious." He grins at my sister. It's odd to have a conversation with someone who is only partly in tune to you or the rest of the room. It's adorable how into one another the two of them are.

Lainey pecks at his lips. "You're delicious."

"You're delicious," he counters with a guttural laugh, and soon they migrate onto the dance floor, feasting off one another's flesh for all to see.

A strong, spiced cologne comes up on me, and I know who it is without having to turn around.

"Lemon."

"If it isn't my favorite judge." I turn with a giddy grin already pinned to my lips. "Rumor has it, you still live next door to me."

"Does that rumor also relay the fact every other judge at the courthouse is somehow out sick this month? I'm a one-man show these days, and I'm not happy about it."

"Ooh, an unhappy judge does not a light sentencing make."

"That is correct. They don't call me the Grinch for nothing."

Naomi struts over in her ultra-short red velvet dress, her long black boots that cover her knees, and a sequin Santa hat pressed over her long dark hair. "Did I hear a handsome someone refer-encing himself as the Grinch?" Her finger flicks over his chin, and something in me burns with the seemingly innocent action. Most likely because I know Naomi all too well to realize there isn't an innocent bone in her body. If only she were a suspect in Tanner's murder, I would have this case on lock and I'd be happily bouncing on a mattress with Noah, getting my cookies frosted real good.

Her mouth falls open as she offers him a coy wink. "You're not the one responsible for all those package thefts, are you?"

A rumble comes from his chest, no smile. Everett really is a master of maintaining that stone-cold mystique. It's more than his charm. It's a part of his soul.

"Not I," he says before nodding my way. "And I've yet to thank you, Lemon. Noah called and let me know what you did. That was admirable. That package was for you, by the way. I'll come over with some wrapping paper, and it can reside in its proper home until Christmas."

"Aw, thank you. Hey, I thought they caught the people?" I look to Naomi. "You haven't had any recent thefts, have you?"

She shakes her head. "I've heard of them as recent as this morning. Mutton says there were three on his block alone."

"That's terrible. That's *criminal.*"

Lily comes up, looking like a naughty Mrs. Claus with her short frilly red dress with its white feathered boa trim.

"Do you know what's criminal?" She sashays right into

Everett's arms. "The fact you're not dancing with anyone —namely me."

Lily looks like a supermodel on any given day, but right now, with her hair wild and curled into her perfect little ringlets, her makeup sparkling as if she were an extraterrestrial inspecting our planet, well, it only magnifies her beauty. As much I appreciate her help around the bakery, I don't much appreciate her helping herself to Everett so liberally. It's like every time I look out the window at night her car is tucked in his driveway. If he trots her off to the dance floor, I might just vomit. Everett doesn't strike me as one who likes to trip the light fantastic.

"I was just thinking the same thing." Everett's lips curve with devious intent. "But Lemon begged me to save the first dance for her."

He takes ahold of my hand and I'm whisked to the dance floor, our bodies so close you can't squeeze a thin dime between us.

"Sorry," he whispers, his hips moving in time with mine.

"For what? My hips haven't had this much action in years."

He belts out a short-lived laugh on his ex-stepbrother's behalf. "I'm glad to oblige."

My favorite red-eyed pooch swoops his way over, his thick, glossy blond hair billowing behind him, and soon he's on two legs trying to cut in.

"Dutch is insistent that I dance with him." I nod over to where he is, and Everett offers a wry smile.

"Tell him to wait in line."

"Very funny. So that big box is really for me? You didn't have to do that."

"Don't thank me yet. It's not entirely for you."

"Ooh, now I'm intrigued. Is this for Noah, too? Are you bequeathing us our first couples gift?"

Before he can answer, Lily taps me over the shoulder, and I'm booted to the side like a cold slice of three-day old pizza.

That's fine. I have cookie platters to replenish. My mother's instincts were on point. Those Christmas tree crunchies have been a mega hit, but they still pale in comparison to how fast those gingerbread men are moving.

I bump into a body on my way out and end up twirling back to the dance floor in Hook Redwood's arms.

"Fancy meeting you here, Lottie." His chest thunders with a dull laugh, and I can feel the rhythm permeating me. Hook is a looker on a regular day, but wearing his Sunday best, his hair slicked back to perfection, he looks as if he should be right back in New York City—modeling underwear in Times Square.

A bubbling laugh escapes me. "Yes, well, I am in charge of the evening's desserts. Have you had one of my cookies?"

His brows lift an inch. "That sounds far more enticing than I'm sure you meant it. Rumor has it, you're taken. Tell me it isn't true."

Another chortling laugh brews in my chest. "It's as true as the truth can get. If only we could find the time to see one another. So, how's the real estate world treating you? Is it a big adjustment?" Hey? Maybe if I can get Hook to cop to his brother's murder, my calendar might actually see Noah's name on it in the very near future. I wince at the thought. Nothing would be more tragic than if Hook did the deed.

"It's going. I guess I have a knack for pushing houses after all." He shakes his head with a faraway look in his eyes. "I just wish my brother was around to help out. When we were kids, we used to pretend we were large and in charge, and now that the reins have been handed to us—I just wish he was around to see it. Rachel has decided to help out. Once she has the baby, she wants to be hands-on."

"Really? What about your father? I thought he had a sons-only policy that you needed to adhere to."

"He did until he was suddenly down a son. But he wants to retire. He made sure my sister was fine with being a working mother. As horrible as his sons-only policy was, he didn't want Rachel missing out on her child's life. But she assured him she was fine with it."

"That's great. I'm sure the two of you will set the world on fire."

A hard tap lands over my shoulder, and I turn to find a scowling Naomi Turner glaring at me.

"You've met your quota on handsome men. Now scoot!" She gives me a hearty sway of the hip, and I end up stumbling my way toward the exit.

The hallway just outside the main hall is nothing more than a dark corridor that leads to the rear of the establishment and the kitchen. I'm about to head over when I spot Ned Sweeny and that creepy kid he keeps stapled to his arm. Next to him stands Bella Carter, whom I now know is his stepdaughter.

Maybe I should go over and say hello? Maybe I should shake them both and have them confess to Tanner's murder whether they did it or not so Noah and I can get on with our nonexistent sex lives. I'm about halfway there when Bella's voice hikes to its upper octave.

"Now that I know the truth, I'll make sure my mother does, too." She darts past me into the crowded room, and my heart thumps wildly. I bet that was about his affair with Kelly! Ned Sweeny is such a moron to think he wouldn't get caught.

I take a few steps in his direction, but he still looks pretty steamed, so I decide to take a right instead.

"Ms. Lemon." His voice reaches out and touches me in every creepy way you can imagine.

I pivot slowly on my heels and offer a meager wave.

Ned's lips expand a moment. The dummy on his wrist slumps as if Ned forgot he was there. "Good evening."

"Hi, Ned. It's nice to see both you and Darjeeling here tonight. Will you be performing?"

His eyes widen a notch. "We were, but Darjeeling isn't feeling well." His features harden.

Oh crap. Why do I sense trouble?

Dutch bounds over and weaves between us as if he weren't feeling well either.

I clear my throat. "I saw Bella storm away. Is everything okay?"

His eyes remain trained on mine a moment too long. "Everything is fine." He lifts his chin, and his arm bucks as he struggles to readjust the doll. A tangle of fine silver tinsel catches the light as it dangles from the fabric that connects his suit with the matching one that Darjeeling wears. He showed it to me that first night at the community center, a piece of cloth that covers the fact his hand is traveling up Darjeeling's back. He described it as an extra coattail that attaches to the dummy's matching suit.

I take a step forward. "I'm afraid you have a bit of a tinsel ball forming." I lift my fingers to free it and gasp. That's not tinsel. That's white curly hair from a very bad wig— A very bad *wig*? Perhaps even the wig that Tanner was wearing that night!

I look up at him with a breath caught in my throat. His eyes are still trained on mine, just as wide and wild as we each have our own revelation.

"You did it," I whisper, and just as quick as the words leave my mouth, Ned Sweeny leaves the Evergreen.

Dutch lets out a riotous bark, and Ned pauses and jerks as if he heard it, too.

I follow him through the crowded entry and into the great white tent with all of those beautifully decorated trees being inspected by potential bidders.

My fingers quickly work over my phone as I put a call into Noah. Music blares from a set of oversized outdoor speakers as "Jingle Bell Rock" vibrates its cheery tune through the night at top volume. I can't hear a thing on my phone, and I'm starting to lose Ned, so I tuck my cell back into my pocket.

I spot Ned's dark hair bobbing through the thicket of people streaming their way into the tent, but he shoots past them and heads for the parking lot instead. Behind the lot the woods lie thick and dark. He could run miles in just about any direction and never get caught. Or at least until the spring thaw. It's a death wish if he tries to run. I do my best to navigate past the crowd, panting as I race into the lot, but I don't see a sign of Ned anywhere.

The sound of incessant barking lights up the night. It's Dutch. I do my best to follow it along and, sure enough, I spot Ned weaving his way through the back of the parking lot.

"Ned, wait," I shout as he pins himself between a black sedan and a silver Buick.

A silver Buick! It looks identical to the one the package thieves used as a getaway car. But that's for another day.

Ned Sweeny and I stand within ten feet of one another. The holiday music is so riotously loud it vibrates the windows of the cars surrounding us, but it's dampened enough for me to hear Ned's own erratic breathing.

"You didn't stab Tanner with that icicle that night. I know that you're innocent of that." My heart slams against my chest like a convict whose prison cell just caught fire.

His forehead smooths away its wrinkles, and he takes a quick breath of relief.

"It was Bella, wasn't it?"

He inches back as if I caught him off guard. "Bella?" He looks to the Evergreen Manor as if he were seeing it for the very first time. "It wasn't Kelly?"

I suck in a sharp breath as the pieces start to fall together. "You thought it was Dr. Ferdinand?" I look to the acrylic hair still clinging to his jacket. The last part of Tanner that can speak from the grave. "You—you had that cloth close enough to his wig to pull the hair right off. My goodness, you smothered him with it—didn't you?" I point to the elongated coattail floating down the dummy's back. "You killed him after you thought Kelly killed him. But it makes no sense."

"It makes sense." He closes his eyes a moment.

I suck in a quick breath. "Because she didn't kill him. She tried, and if he survived, he would have implicated her"—my mouth widens—"and outed you. But it wasn't Kelly. It was Bella. Would you have done it for her if you knew?"

"I did, didn't I?" He plucks his arm free and shoves Darjeeling at me so hard it nearly knocks me to the ground.

Ned bolts for the great white tent, and Dutch bounds right after him.

"That's right, boy"—I pant as I do my best to keep up—"stay on him."

Inside the oversized tent it's brightly lit, the sound of laughter mingles with the powerfully loud Christmas carols belting out overhead, and it's a miracle people aren't passing out from the rumbling of the bass alone.

Each of the hundreds of trees is delicately decorated from head to toe in a specific theme—an under the sea extravaganza, an Americana delight, the ode to baking catches my eye, and that tree that features a bevy of feathered masks that my sister has her eye on. Near the back, a twelve-foot noble nearly capsizes, and my guess is that it has to do with a nervous murder suspect who's just been outed. I speed in that direction and the barking picks up.

It's sparse of both trees and people this far back in the tent, and I spot Ned's boots walking slowly behind a tree festooned with fishing gear, small poles, hooks, and long metal lures in a rainbow of colors, some with plastic skirts that give them the appeal of a squid.

"You did it for love," I say, my voice shaking. "I get it, Ned. And the sheriff will understand that, too. You're not the first person to get caught up in the heat of the moment. You can plead momentary insanity." Or long-term, judging by how he chooses to spend his downtime.

Ned steps out of the shadows, his chin tucked toward his chest, his eyes still very much pinned on mine.

My word, he looks absolutely out of his mind. And I must be the same to have chased him this way. Dutch leaps supernaturally in and out of the tree between us as if he couldn't be bothered to interrupt his good time with the standoff I'm currently embroiled in.

"It's true," Ned says it low with a growl. "I never intended for that to happen. I was in a blind panic when I saw her leave and him lying there in the snow. I knew she didn't kill him. I couldn't risk him telling Hannah. He would be furious with Kelly when he came to. But Kelly—she's innocent." He shakes his head as if coming to himself. "I'm leaving tonight, Lottie. Just stay out of my way and you'll never see me again."

I'm about to make a run for it myself when his eyes widen at something behind me, but before I can turn around, Ned has my back against his chest, the business end of one of those lures pinching at my neck. He's holding me so tight I can hardly catch my next breath.

Noah stands before us, his hand on his back before he slowly raises both hands, empty of any weapon.

Ned jerks me back as he drags us toward an opening in the tent. "Stay there or she gets hurt!" he shouts to Noah. And unfortunately for me, Noah does as he's told.

A patrol car rolls up into the lot, and Ned speeds us back deeper into the tent.

"Freeze!" Noah shouts, his weapon already drawn. His eyes are laser-focused on Ned's. The muscles in his jaw pop as do those biceps and, my goodness, I think I'm far more attracted to Noah at this inopportune moment than I've ever been before, and that's saying a lot. And if I can manage not to get my throat slit, I predict we'll be having our own rockin' Christmas Eve—but hopefully much, much sooner, like say *tonight*.

Maybe I can convince Ned that I'm on his side, be the liaison between him and that Glock Noah has pointed our way?

"He didn't mean to—"

"Shut up!" Ned tenses beneath me, and that metal hook he has pinching my neck feels as if it just took a bite out of me. "I'm taking her with me," he shouts to Noah, and Noah's eyes expand with a level of rage I've never seen in them before. Okay, well, maybe once before when he was dealing with Everett, but this budding rage is all due to how much he loves me and I'm finding it very vexingly attractive. It's safe to say my body is begging to put an end to this Darjeeling sponsored drought. Hey, that dummy really did cramp my style!

Ned gives me a violent yank as he drags me back behind the fishing themed tree. He hoists me up on his hip as if I were one of his wooden idiots and I try to break free, but that hook feels as if it's about to rip out a vocal cord or two.

Noah steps around the tree carefully and am I ever glad to see his scruff-peppered face again.

Ned bucks beneath me. "I said stay back! My car is in the lot. I'll leave her here if you don't follow. I won't take her with me." His voice shakes as he inches his way toward the crowd. I'm not sure either Noah or I believe him.

Dutch bounds at us from out of nowhere, barking and growling, his crimson eyes spasming like flares.

"He did it for love," I say to Noah, hoping Ned will want to stick around long enough for the rest of the sheriff's department to join in on the fun.

"You're right," Ned pants close to my ear. "Kelly and I had a good thing. We weren't hurting anybody. She left Mason because it wasn't right that she was seeing the two of us. He's my stepson, for Pete's sake. But she chose me and I knew she would. We have something special. Something Hannah could never give me."

"So, why not leave her? Why cheat on your poor wife?" I shout up at him. I'm pretty sure if a madman has a hook to your throat it's a pretty lousy time to get in an argument with him.

The razor-sharp tip scratches at my flesh. "Kelly and I were happy just the way things were. Enough of that." He wraps his arms around me.

"Is that why you smothered Tanner? Because he was going to ruin your good thing?" Of course, he's all but confessed to me, but it'd be a nice touch if I could get him to pipe up for Noah as well.

"I said enough!" Ned riots into my ear, and Dutch snarls and snaps as he jumps right through both Ned Sweeny and me.

Ned staggers backward, taking me with him, and before we know it, Noah is on us, freeing me from Ned's grasp as he wrestles him to the ground.

In an instant, this desolate end of the tent is filled with men in blue, weapons drawn, until Ned is finally cuffed and helped to his feet. A crowd has amassed, women are screaming, and Dutch is doing an odd complication of backflips and cartwheels.

Ned looks my way and shakes his head. "How did you know? How did you know I had anything to do with this at all?"

"Call it a hunch, call it my thirst for justice, or call it the fact you had half of Tanner's wig hanging from your arm."

Noah comes at me and pulls me into a monstrous hug.

"But mostly, it had to do with a very real need to end one serious dry spell."

Noah brushes a kiss to my lips as they haul Ned away. "I smell rain."

"Not quite yet." I relay everything regarding Bella to the sheriff's deputies in our midst, and they take off for the Evergreen. By the time we hit the entrance, Bella is being escorted out with her hands behind her back, her amber curls falling over her face every which way.

Her eyes hook to mine, and she takes a few steps in our direction. "I didn't mean it." She shakes her head at me. "I knew that night at the restaurant that you were onto me, and I almost told you everything then. He just got me so mad. When I saw him with that other girl—the same girl that was seeing my brother, I just lost it. I grabbed an icicle off the ground and followed him into the field. I wanted to fight, but he said he needed to get away. There was never enough time for me—so I did it. I pierced his neck. As soon as he saw red, Tanner passed out. He never could stand the sight of blood. I took off, too."

"That's when you hit your stepfather's minivan." I nod as if affirming the fact.

"How did you know that? Were you watching me the entire time?"

"And Ned didn't make a big deal out of it because he thought it might have been Kelly speeding out of the lot."

"He thought Kelly stabbed Tanner?" She shakes her head. "But I thought he did that for me. I told him tonight I was going to confess everything to my mother. He got so upset. He must have thought I was outing his affair." She closes her eyes a moment. "I never meant to hurt Tanner. I'm so sorry."

They take her away toward the same lot I had chased Ned Sweeny in just a little while ago, and a thought comes to me.

"Noah, that silver Buick—the getaway vehicle from the

package thefts, I'm pretty sure it's out there. I saw it myself. It's in the back," I shout to a nearby deputy, and he assures us he'll check it out.

Noah rumbles with a quiet laugh as his gaze penetrates mine. "Lottie Lemon, is there anything you can't do?"

I bite down on a smile. "Yes, I can't seem to find any alone time with you."

Noah winces, and suddenly it's clear to me that tonight isn't looking so hot either.

"*Fox!*" an all too familiar female voice shrills from behind, and I glance over his shoulder to find Detective Ivy Fairbanks looking both stunning and angry in a long red coat. "We need to process these suspects now. There's a mountain of paperwork to be done tonight."

"I'll be right there. I'm just taking a statement from a crucial eyewitness." He presses a kiss over my lips, and it warms me straight to my toes. "It sounds like I'll be working late tonight."

"I know. Tomorrow's Christmas Eve. Try to pencil in that dinner at the B&B." I'd give a playful wink, but there's not anything playful about it. "When will I see you again?"

"Soon." He backs up, and that serious as death expression lets me know he means it. "Real soon."

But something tells me it's not soon enough.

CHAPTER 19

*C*hristmas Eve at my mother's bed and breakfast is a sight to behold. The cavernous dining room is festooned with twinkle lights and a grand blue noble in the corner that stands ten feet tall bejeweled with ornaments that span our entire family history. There are baubles of every shape and size dangling from each branch, and an animatronic angel sits on top, opening and closing her wings in a rainbow of fiber optic light. The tablecloth is candy apple red, and my mother has her gold chargers on display—on top of each of those sits my grandmother's fine china with the holly pattern encircling each dish like a wreath.

Stockings are hung above the fireplace, and a small mountain of gifts wait patiently for Christmas morning tucked under the tree. The B&B has drained of all its holiday guests, and it's just my mother, Mr. Rutherford—I may have frowned at him more than once this evening, Lainey and Forest, Keelie, Naomi, their mother Becca and their grandmother Nell, and, of course, Everett and Noah who each sit dutifully on either side of me. The three of us actually drove out together and a war didn't break out. Go figure.

A soft bark emits from near the tree as Dutch looks to me while happily attempting to chew on the packages. And thankfully, Dutch seems to be sticking around, too, although I may never know why. But I'm glad about it.

I look to Everett and Noah, and I can't help but smile as the last of our feast lands on the table. I'm glad about a lot of things.

Lainey stands to her feet and lifts her glass. "I would like to give a toast—to a wonderful Christmas with family and friends. I can't think of a better way to spend the holidays than with everyone in this very room."

The rest of us lift our glasses and give a unanimous cheer.

"And"—she holds a finger up, and the room grows quiet once again—"to my sweet and slightly certifiable sister, Lottie. Thank you for giving me, and I think I speak for all of us here, thank you for giving all of us a wonderful gift—the gift of getting some decent shut-eye." The room breaks out into a warm laugh. "You not only have a knack for finding dead bodies, you have a knack for bringing their killer to justice"—she looks to Forest, and her cheeks pinch pink—"and perhaps a knack for reuniting old flames."

Forest stands, and they share a tender kiss.

Sometimes things do go as planned in life. You have an argument, you end up with the wrong person, but seasons change. Fate and destiny interweave their plans for you, and if you can manage to escape the suspect list of an active homicide investigation, then you just might find yourself in the arms where you've belonged all along. It sure worked out for my sister.

Noah wraps an arm around me, and I lean against him with a dreamy look in my eyes.

And it worked for me.

Dinner goes off without a hitch, without anyone throwing a dinner roll at anyone else—and, believe you me, both Mr. Rutherford and his wandering hands had me tempted. Dessert is served, a traditional Yule log I've been gracing our Christmas table with for years, and, of course, a platter of my now infamous gingerbread cookies.

Soon, the table is cleared and bodies are mingling around the room.

"Mom, Lainey"—I say as the three of us congregate near the fire—"I have a gift for you, Mom, but it's not exactly from me." I give my sister a sly wink as I hand the small gold box with a shiny red bow on it to our mother.

"What in heavens?" Mom peels off the bow and opens the box, her mouth contorting in every shape and size. "Oh my." Her voice quivers as she pulls the silver ring out of the box. "Oh, Lottie, how did you ever?"

"Consider it a Christmas miracle."

Lainey and I admire our father's ring as Mom quickly works it onto the chain dangling from her neck.

"He'll be right here"—she pats her chest—"next to my heart where he belongs." A tear rolls down her cheek as Lainey and I offer her a hearty embrace.

The Christmas carols pick up, and the mood in the room shifts to something more jovial as we continue to mingle.

Keelie traipses up with a small red bag. "I've got a little something for you!"

"Keelie! No gifts, remember? I thought we said we were going to take one another shopping in Ashford for all the after Christmas sales?"

"We are, but I thought you might need this sooner." She thrusts the bag my way.

"What is it?" I carefully extract its contents before shoving them right back in. "*Keelie!*" I can't even pretend to be mad at her. "How did you know?" I pull it out just enough to ogle at the tiny nightie that would make St. Nicholas' ruby red cheeks remain flushed for a year. "I love it. Thank you."

"Oh, honey, it's not for you. It's for Noah."

"Well then, I thank you on his behalf."

"Besides, you lost the first one. It's the least I could do." She wrinkles her nose over my shoulder, and I follow her gaze to where Naomi is all but tackling Everett.

"I see a man sending out an SOS if ever there was one." She bites down on her lower lip seductively. "Excuse me while I rescue me a tall, handsome legal eagle. You'd better hide that nightie from me or I might just snap it up for myself." She takes off with a wiggle in her hips, and I'm about to make my way to Noah before Nell hobbles my way and blocks me off at the pass. Nell will be ninety-three in January, and I can't wait to help celebrate her birthday with her. She doesn't know it, but Becca is planning to host a giant bash at the Honey Pot Diner.

"Merry Christmas, dear one." She lands a kiss to my cheek, and Dutch hops up as if he wanted one of his own. She turns to him and chortles. "Oh, goodness. You are a lively one, aren't you?"

I'm about to laugh and agree when suddenly the air is knocked right out of my lungs.

"You can see him!"

Nell looks up, her mouth agape, her eyes set wide. "Oh me, oh my." She lifts her hand to her mouth and seals it. "I'm sorry,

Lottie. I should have told you sooner." She looks over her shoulder as Becca comes over with Nell's coat extended.

"Goodnight, Lottie." Becca gifts me a warm embrace. "I'm afraid it's past my bedtime. Yours, too, Mother." She helps Nell with her coat and begins hustling her away.

"*Nell*," I say, shaking my head, stymied by what's just happened.

Nell takes a step back and grabs ahold of my arm, her head inching toward mine. "It's time I told you everything, child."

"Mother"—Becca rolls her eyes with a jolly laugh bouncing from her chest—"you can tell Lottie all the stories you want after the big day tomorrow. William is coming into town, and we need to get up early to start the turkey if we plan on eating at three."

"Oh, you." Nell is quick to wave her off, before reverting her full attention back to me. "I promise you, dear." Her pale eyes fill with tears. "I will tell you everything. No truth will I withhold from you any longer. It's high time you knew," she whispers before the two of them head for the exit.

Noah breaks away from Mr. Rutherford and wraps his arms around me. "Everything okay? You look as if you just saw a ghost."

I glance past him at Dutch who has resumed the task of trying to open the gifts himself.

"A ghost. Imagine that?"

We head out ourselves, and Everett joins us as we take off and head for Country Cottage Road, for home.

NOAH PARKS IN MY DRIVEWAY, and the three of us—four of us if you count one rambunctious Golden Retriever—amble out, and I invite Everett in because I happen to have a gift for him.

"You parked in her driveway." Everett ticks his head toward Noah. "Did you pencil that in last week?"

Noah growls, and I can't get the door open fast enough. We burst in, and I turn on the lights, rousing Pancake from the luxurious nap he was having on the sofa.

"I have a gift for you," I say, looking to Everett as I turn on the twinkle lights wrapped around the tree, and the room explodes in holiday wonder.

"I'll start a fire," Noah volunteers as I fish the small package out from under the Douglas fir, which seems to be losing needles at an alarming rate. It's safe to say there are actually more needles on the floor than on the branches, but thankfully neither Pancake nor I are bothered by it.

"Here you go." I hand the small red box to Everett, and Dutch hops up onto the sofa as if wanting to see it for himself. "I insist you go first."

Everett lifts a brow as he looks to Noah. "Take note, Fox. I'm her first of the night." He unwraps the package with ease and opens the lid to the small box, revealing a pair of sterling silver cufflinks.

"Ah, yes." His lips curve upright for a moment.

"Apparently, a man in demand such as yourself can't have enough of those. Don't give those to Lily." It still makes me roll my eyes that she convinced him that giving a girl your cufflinks was the new class ring. Who knows what she's doing with those cufflinks at night? If I were him, I wouldn't want them back.

"Are you kidding? These are from you." He lifts the box my way. "It works both ways, you know. I guess this makes us a thing."

Noah groans, "You're a thing, all right. Ever hear of the phrase *three's a crowd?*"

"Oh, wait!" I say, pulling up the box that Everett came over this afternoon to wrap. I made him cocoa, and we sat by the fire talking about our favorite gifts we received as a child. Mine was a doll almost as tall as I was at the time, and his was a scooter on which he promptly broke his leg and decided to go somewhere safe like law school. "Let's see what's in here." I give Everett a wink. "The girl equivalent of cufflinks?"

I unwrap the box and burst on into it—pulling up—"A cushion?" I say, trying to make heads or tails out of the pale blue— "*Bed!*" I shout as I hold it out and inspect it in a whole new light.

"That's right. It's a bed for Pancake. It's terrifying to see that poor cat trying to balance himself on the armrest. This way he gets his own space. Everyone needs their own space. Isn't that right, dude?" Everett scratches Pancake behind the ears, and I don't know what's funnier—the fact Pancake is purring like a jet engine or the fact Everett just called him dude.

"Speaking of space." Noah stands next to me as a devious grin glides over his face as he stares down Everett. "Don't you have a place of your own?"

"You're subtle. I like that." Everett glares at him a moment. "Merry Christmas."

Noah reaches out and shakes his hand, and something about the action warms me. "Merry Christmas, Everett. Please extend the holiday greeting to your mother and sister tomorrow."

"I will." Everett heads to the door, and I walk him out as Noah tosses in a few extra logs into the fire. I step out onto the porch and offer Everett a firm embrace.

"Merry Christmas, Everett. I hope you find everything you want in that stocking of yours once you wake up."

A soft chuckle bounces from him. "Same to you. Merry Christmas, Lemon."

I give a quick glance over my shoulder. "There's something I have to tell you," I whisper. "She saw him tonight. Nell Sawyer saw Dutch with her own two eyes!"

"What?" he hisses, inspecting me as if I've lost my mind all over again.

"Yes. And she said she's going to tell me everything once Christmas is behind us."

"Lottie, this is great. It sounds as if you're going to get the answers you've been looking for."

"I know. I can't believe it. This is really turning out to be the best Christmas ever."

"That's great." He glances over my shoulder back into the brightly lit house. His lips purse, and he looks decidedly angry for a moment. "So, you and Noah, huh?"

"Oh, right"—I say awkwardly, hitching my thumb back at the living room—"we're you know..."

"Finalizing plans."

"Yes, that." My cheeks burn with the heat of ten thousand suns.

"Tonight." He nods stoically as if he's coming to terms with something horrible.

"Yes, um. I guess, tonight."

"You sure he's the one?" Everett needles me with those cobalt blue eyes. He's penetrating me right down to my soul as if he were trying to subliminally rouse me from a terrible dream.

"Yes." I shake my head as I look to him. "Everett, are you trying to say something?" My heart jumps in my chest at the thought of what might come from his mouth next.

"No." He swallows hard, and his eyes cast to the ground a moment. "But just so you know, you shook your head when you said yes. In a courtroom, I would have assumed you were lying." He turns to leave, and Dutch bounds out of the house and follows Everett down the walk.

"Oh—it looks as if Dutch is following you home," I shout after him.

"Can't blame him." Everett waves with a lift of his hand as he makes his way up the street. "He doesn't want to stick around for the carnage. He's welcome to spend the night."

Noah reels me in as we seal ourselves back inside. "Who's welcome to spend the night?" he asks as he dots my lips with a kiss.

"*You.*" I lift a shoulder as I reach past him to that bag Keelie gave me.

"What's that?"

"Something from Keelie and me to you." I wrinkle my nose as I mention my bestie during what's about to be a very intimate moment.

"A gift to me from two women? This night only gets better." His dimples dig in, and my stomach drops through the floor. I can't believe I get this handsome man all to myself.

"You bet it does." I pull it out and hold the frilly frock between us, and a dark laugh pumps from him.

"It is going to be a very Merry Christmas, Lottie Lemon. But first, I have something for you." He pulls out a small navy box with a miniature red bow sitting on top of it.

"Noah! The only thing I have for you is, well, me." I lift a shoulder with a coy smile. "I might have a T-shirt that says *I belong to the baker*, but it's really for Ivy." I smack my lips as if I were going to be sick at the mention of her name.

Noah bucks with a silent laugh as he hands me the box and I lift the lid, exposing a pair of diamond stud earrings.

He pulls my hand up and kisses it. "I thought they sparkled like your eyes."

"Noah, it's too much."

"It's not enough," he says as I struggle to take my eyes off them.

"You're enough." I hike up on my tiptoes and crash my mouth to his, suddenly hungry for something that couldn't be found on that buffet spread my mother had out tonight.

Noah and I amble our way back to the bedroom, our kisses growing in ferocity. I land the earrings down onto the kitchen counter as we pass it by, and my fingers rake open his shirt.

His eyes remain trained on mine as he gives a dark laugh. "Turnabout is fair play," he says as he lifts my sweater right off.

"I don't think I'm going to get a chance to wear this nightie," I say, tossing it over my shoulder.

"It's the thought that counts," he says as he sweeps me off my feet and into his arms.

"Why do I get the feeling things are about to get a little wild and out of hand?"

A dirty smile glides over his lips. "Let's just say I'm not a baker. When I frost cookies, things tend to get messy. And believe me when I say I plan to be highly creative with the endeavor."

"How creative, detective?"

Noah belts out a laugh as he carries us into my bedroom, the bed already drawn in anticipation. You might say I was hopeful this afternoon. The battery-operated candles are flickering away —hey, a girl can't burn her house down while she's at her mother's—and the scent of the cinnamon wreath hanging over my bed gives the air just the right amount of spice it needs on a night like tonight.

"Let's just say Everett may have given Pancake something to purr about, but I'm about to make you sing."

"Oh?" I can't help but giggle. "Is this your way of saying your package is bigger than his?"

A dark laugh strums from him "There are some things you should find out for yourself."

I swipe the Santa hat off my dresser that's been a part of my uniform down at the bakery for the entire month of December.

I run my finger along Noah's strong jawline and over his lips. "I sure hope Santa fills my stocking to the brim tonight."

The idea of a dark laugh strums from him as he lands the hat over his head.

"Brace yourself, Cupcake. I'm about to frost your cookies."

Noah shuts the door with his foot, and we spend the rest of the evening conducting a very thorough investigation of everything we've ever wanted to know about one another—many, many times in a savory night.

Suffice it to say, this officially goes down as the best Christmas ever.

PICK up Seven-Layer Slayer (Murder in the Mix 5) and read NOW! Turn the page for a preview and Enjoy!

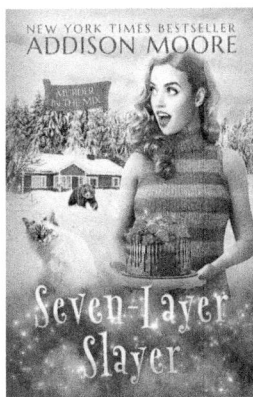

PREVIEW: Seven-Layer Slayer

My name is Lottie Lemon, and I see dead people. Okay, so I rarely see dead people. Mostly I see furry creatures of the dearly departed variety, who have come back from the other side to warn me of their previous owner's impending doom.

It's January, and this month brings two special birthdays

that the entire town is looking forward to celebrating: Eve Hollister and Nell Sawyer's. Well, in truth, not many people are looking forward to celebrating Eve Hollister's birthday. In fact, the way the people at her party are acting, you'd think she were the most hated woman on the planet. Add one ornery black bear who is well past his earthly prime, along with the Grim Reaper, and poor Eve's birthday turns into a supernatural catastrophe. One thing is for sure—no one in Honey Hollow will ever be the same.

LOTTIE LEMON HAS a brand new bakery to tend to, a budding romance with perhaps one too many suitors, and she has the supernatural ability to see dead pets—which are always harbingers for ominous things to come. Throw in the occasional ghost of the human variety, a string of murders, and her insatiable thirst for justice, and you'll have more chaos than you know what to do with.

Living in the small town of Honey Hollow can be murder.

Chapter 1

I see dead people.

Okay, so it's very, very rare, but I do seem to see creatures of the furry dearly departed variety on the regular. And, believe you me, it is never a good sign to their previous owner. It is always a harbinger of terrible things to come. Up until a few months ago, the horror used to amount to nothing more than a scraped knee or a horrible tumble. But these days, it almost always amounts to death.

Just a few weeks ago, Tanner Redwood's Golden Retriever, Dutch, bounded back into reality—my reality anyhow. Apparently, I'm the only one with vision that extends right into eternity. Wait—that's not entirely true. I just recently discovered that my best friend's Grammy Nell can see these fantastic phantasms, too. But anyhow, Dutch was the first creature that I not only saw but *heard*. He's a beauty with long golden hair, wears a smile for most of the day, and loves to cuddle with my Himalayan cat, Pancake.

I'm pretty sure Pancake can't see or hear him, but he definitely senses a disturbance in the force. It's probably best Pancake, nor anyone else can see the majestic beast—aside from his transparent qualities, he has eyes that blaze like fire, and it's really quite alarming. Aside from that, Dutch is the first furry phantasm that has not disappeared after his owner's murder was solved. Strangely enough, he's taken up firm residency in my living room.

"Lottie!" Mom waves to me, frantic as an entire herd of women stream into the oversized living room of the B&B. It's not only the day that her historical book club meets up for the month, but it also happens to be the birthday of the founder, Eve Hollister. "Lottie, please make sure the dessert buffet is kept well replenished." She jabs a finger to an elongated table near the entry of the room that I've laden with every sweet treat that the Cutie Pie Bakery and Cakery could muster. It's especially laden down with Eve's favorites, like the chocolate chip peanut butter swirl cookies, dark chocolate dreams, and rocky road brownies. Eve Hollister has had a sweet tooth for as long as I've known her.

"Will do!" I note the brownies are running low and head to the kitchen to replenish the supply.

I'm not halfway there before I come upon the birthday girl herself, Eve Hollister, and a couple of her guests. Eve is actually the same age as my mother, but she's had a rough go of it, and unfortunately looks as if she could be my mother's mother. In Eve's defense, my mother has found the fountain of youth and is willing to deny its existence until her dying day.

Miranda Lemon looks like she could be in magazines with her shoulder-length butter yellow locks, her svelte physique—

and the fact she is always overdressed for any and every occasion doesn't hurt either. I'm convinced my mother came out of the womb looking impeccably put together.

In contrast, Eve looks like your stereotypical grandmother with short white hair, a hobble to her step, and wrinkles worn proud like a badge well earned. Both Eve and my mother lost their husbands around the same time many years ago. Eve hasn't dated since, that I'm aware of, but my mother has more than made up for it for the both of them. Miranda Lemon has a steady rotation of men she likes to keep warm by her side. As of late, she's dating an abhorrence of an individual, one that happened to be cheating on his ex-wife just a few months back —the same ex-wife who tried to poison him. Brad Rutherford has an insatiable appetite for both women and a wild time— clearly a double whammy of reasons why he should be nowhere near my mother, and I'd go as far as to say no one else's mother either.

The two younger women standing with Eve appear to be locked in a heated argument with the poor frazzled woman, and on this her birthday. They have a familiar look, and I can't quite put my finger on where I know them. One girl looks to be about my age but far more polished, with her chocolate brown hair slicked back into a bun, her pencil skirt and heels both something I would eschew. I'm more of a pony, jeans, and sweater girl myself. My cozy shearling boots are perfect for running around the bakery and making deliveries this frozen time of year.

January in Honey Hollow, Vermont rarely calls for stilettos, but you can't tell my sister Lainey that or apparently this woman either. The other girl locked in the heated debate looks younger, with pleasant wide-set features that would appeal to any man, a shock of red lipstick, and sleek glossy hair dyed a jarring shade of silver.

The one with gray locks leans in—it's an ironic hair color,

considering the fact she looks younger than I do at twenty-six. "You won't get away with this forever."

The brunette is quick to wave off the ingénue. "You know, ever since Daddy died, she's been tighter than those shrunken jeans you're wearing. You can't teach an old horse new tricks."

"It's *dog*," the younger one corrects.

"Woof woof," Eve bleats with a laugh.

I try to boot scoot my way past them, and Eve's eyes light up like that Christmas tree my mother still has lit up in the corner.

"Lottie Lemon!" she cries. "You remember my girls, Daphne and Brenda Lee?" She points to the uptight brunette and the angry gray-haired girl respectively.

"Oh my goodness," I say, stunned as both girls glare back at me as if I've just let a noxious odor fly. Upon closer inspection, I do see traces of Eve in their features. Both are wildly attractive. The brunette, Daphne, has that nude makeup palate look going, and with her upscale skirt and navy silk blouse, she looks elegantly understated.

Brenda Lee has a boho chic vibe with a jacket that looks as if it was made out of a psychedelic quilt, and a sweater that looks as if someone ripped off the midsection, which would explain why it's unraveling at the base—a purposeful look, I'm tragically sure —and let's not forget the aforementioned shrunken jeans.

"Yes!" I try to match Eve's enthusiasm, which only makes her daughter's glower all the more in my direction. "I mean, I knew you had children."

The Hollister kids are all about my age, but they were more or less what amounted to an urban legend here in Honey Hollow. We're such a small, close-knit town, that it's a miracle they managed to evade the entire state of Vermont for the duration of their childhood. The three of them—a rumored brother included —all went to boarding school in Switzerland. I believe Eve once mentioned a couple of them live in Ashford now. Too good for Honey Hollow, I suppose.

Eve Hollister herself has more money than she knows what to do with, and she's just as happy to live in Honey Hollow as the rest of us.

"So nice to meet you both. I'm Lottie. I run the bakery on Main Street. If you're ever in the area, please stop by. It would be my pleasure to send you home with a box full of goodies. Our mothers are very good friends."

The younger one smirks and scoffs. "Our mother has *friends*? How much does your mother charge a month?"

The two of them break out into cackles, and my mouth falls open as I look to Eve. Surely they're kidding—right?

Eve winks my way. "Oh, they're just being silly." She offers them a curt smile. "Lottie here was kind enough to bake her famous seven-layer cake for my birthday. It's my absolute favorite."

"I sure did, and it was my pleasure! Four layers of rich decadent chocolate and three with French vanilla. And don't forget the generous layers of Bavarian cream and berries sprinkled on top. It was a feat finding berries in January, but I tracked them down for you. I'm baking the same cake for Nell in just two weeks." Nell Sawyer is my best friend, Keelie Turner's grandmother—*Grammy*. Nell also happens to be the only one I have ever shared my supernatural secret with. Well, I told Everett, my new neighbor, the judge, but he sort of wrangled it out of me.

Regardless, Nell not only knows my secret, but I just discovered this past Christmas Eve that she shares the same gift. She saw and heard Dutch, too. Suffice it to say, I've been itching to have one long sit-down with her ever since that night. No sooner did I discover Nell's own supernatural secret than her daughter shuttled her out the door. Nell promised we'd get together after the holidays, but she's been under the weather as of late so I thought I'd wait until she felt better.

"*Ooh*"—Brenda Lee rolls her eyes—"seven-layer cake." She twirls a finger in the air and makes a crazy face at her sister. "How very creative, Mother."

Wow. Eve Hollister must have inadvertently reared the rudest children—daughters anyway—on the planet. I'm beginning to think it was pure luck I evaded them all these years.

I hold up a finger. "Brenda Lee?" It comes out curt, and I don't mind one bit. "That's a very beautiful name, and I think it indeed proves that your mother is very creative."

"Brenda Lee!" Eve snaps her fingers and dances a spontaneous jig. "She was my favorite singer growing up. Oh, she was just the best."

Brenda Lee shoves her finger down her throat and pretends to gag.

Daphne elbows her. "Would you stop with the theatrics? Let's get this over with." She drags her sister into the living room, and I'm left to shrug at Eve.

"Lovely?" I didn't mean for it to come out a question but, honest to heaven, there was no way around it.

"Just one minute, Lottie." Eve waves me off as someone behind me hijacks her attention. "Well, if it isn't Connie Chutney!" Eve pulls the older woman into a quick embrace. Connie looks like a fitter, and judging by the sour look on her face, a tad more bitter version of Eve.

The older woman grunts. "You just knew I was coming up on my golden badge today, this very day, and you had to have a birthday party," she grits it through her teeth before turning my way. "I'm coming up on the most coveted badge of them all." She turns to Eve with an uncontested look of malice. "Sometimes I think you do these things to me on purpose." She gives Eve's cheek a hard pinch and causes the birthday girl to yelp.

"Yes, well"—a devilish gleam takes over Eve's blue eyes—"a girl must do what a girl must do." Her demeanor changes on a dime as her own expression grows hostile. "Speaking of sabotage, I can't believe you set my article to such a garish background —*crimson* with black ink! And don't you think I didn't notice the fact you made my name far smaller than you did yours. Sometimes I don't know why I bother contributing to the volunteer newsletter."

I try to take a step away from what is obviously a private conversation regarding highly coveted badges that I care to know nothing about and newsletter sabotage, and yet Eve reels me right back in their bickering midst.

"Connie, this is Lottie Lemon. She's *catering* the event for me today. Lottie, this is Connie Chutney. We've volunteered down at the hospital for the last four decades."

Connie extends a bony hand, no smile. "I'm the head volunteer down at Honey Hollow General Hospital. And I'm also in charge of editing the volunteer newsletter. Someone here is just bitter that my articles are better received." She gives a barely-there wink.

Eve balks, "Mine would be better received if people could actually *see* them."

Eve straightens a moment as she looks over my shoulder, and I turn to see Bear and an older man both dressed in jeans and flannels with tool belts slung low on their hips. Otis Fisher—*Bear* as he's better known in these parts, is my infamous ex. We were together for three torturous high school years, but then he decided he wanted more than one girl to torment with his presence. My fragile broken heart when I discovered his pre-teen paramour and I hightailed it out of Honey Hollow and straight to New York City, where I had the rest of my heart smashed to smithereens by the next ex on my list.

I used to have such poor luck with men, I never thought I'd

meet a prince, but, sure enough, last fall I met someone better than your run-of-the-mill next in line for some useless throne—I met a drop-dead gorgeous detective, my fabulous new boyfriend Noah Corbin Fox. My insides detonate just thinking about him.

Noah and I recently took our relationship to the next level, and let's just say that he's been over every single night ready and willing to frost my cookies. And, my goodness, does that man ever know how frost me right into outer space. My entire body is overheating just thinking about it.

"What are they doing here?" Eve gives the construction duo a suspicious look and yanks me right out of my Noah-inspired trance.

Mom bursts into our tiny circle. "Don't you worry about a thing, missy." She slings an arm over Eve's shoulders. "They're here for me. One can never have enough men in the house." She waves them over. "I'm thinking of adding a conservatory—that's a fancy word for sunroom—and Bear offered to give me a free estimate."

"I thought Bill should be here, too." Connie leans in. Her hair is short and curly, a salt and pepper color with salt winning the battle. Her face is round, her wrinkles soft, but by contrast, that hardened expression never seems to leave her. "I figured since he was dropping me off, he might as well place a bid himself." Her eyes narrow as she looks to Eve. "Miranda had to tell me about the addition herself." She pokes Eve hard in the chest. "You know Bill needs the business this time of year. It should have been you who recommended him."

Eve inches back, her lips buttoned up as if she were holding back a deluge of words, not one of them kind. Eve has had an infamous remodel going on now for over a year, and it looks as if she has nothing good to say about Bill and his remodeling skills.

Mom ushers the men off and Connie follows, barking orders to poor Bill who looks as if he wants to be anywhere but here. He offers Eve a curt nod as he passes her by, and just like the rest of her guests, he doesn't seem all that happy to see her. My stars, they all act as if they want to slaughter her in her sleep.

I clear my throat. Despite her foibles, Eve is a kind soul. I think.

"Well, I'm going to make sure you have the best birthday party ever," I say, determined to make it happen.

"That makes two of us!" a cheery voice calls from behind as a stunning blonde bounces her way over and offers Eve an embrace. "Where do you want the gifts, boss?"

Eve waves off the idea of such a generous offering. "How I wish you didn't buy me anything. I don't pay you much to begin with!"

The blonde lifts a brow. "I keep saying if you cut my wages I'd be working for free."

An entire crowd of women heads this way, and Eve makes her way to them.

"Lottie Lemon," I'm quick introduce myself to the only person outside of my mother who I've seen maintain a level of civility toward the birthday girl. "You work for Eve?"

"That's right. I'm Valerie Vernon, modern-day handmaiden, ten ruthless hours a day. No breaks. Eve thinks all I do is sit around. You try cleaning that haunted mansion of hers and see how easy it is. Eve Hollister makes Ebenezer Scrooge look like a prized benefactor." She stalks off, looking far more bitter than she did when she arrived, and I'm at a loss for words. Et tu, Valerie Vernon?

After threading through a sea of limbs, I finally make my way to the kitchen, where I note the fact I left the back door open after hauling in the countless cookie platters.

My mother purchased the B&B the year after she lost my father, and this has been her source of income and her beloved pet project ever since. The kitchen is impressively large and has all the top-of-the-line appliances you could wish for. But nevertheless, I insisted on baking all of my goodies at the Cutie Pie. That bakery is essentially my home away from—

"Oh my word!" I howl so loud my voice reverberates off the walls. Standing next to the opened back door is an eight-foot tall black bear, complete with a menacing growl, angry red mouth, and razor sharp teeth that look as if they were just itching to clamp themselves down over one of my juicy little arms.

The enormous beast rocks back and stands on its hind legs, letting out an egregiously howl—so loud, my eardrums beg to burst from the effort.

My body freezes solid, every muscle I own has turned to stone, and I can't seem to catch my next breath. It takes a lumbering step forward and upturns a couple of empty cookie sheets, sending them to the floor with a clatter before letting out another menacing growl.

"*Lottie?*" Mom stomps her way in, hands on hips, looking visibly annoyed with me. "What in the heck is going on here? It sounds like you're tearing up my kitchen." She heads over and picks the cookie sheets right off the floor and lands them onto the counter where they belong. She turns my way, the bear dwarfing her in size, breathing down her neck as he stands menacingly close behind her. "My goodness! What has gotten into you? You look as if you've seen a ghost."

"A ghost!" I shout so loud it might as well be a cry for help.

The bear stalks its way right through my mother before dropping to all fours and bounding out toward the bustling birthday party.

"*Whew.*" Mom fans herself a moment. "I think I just had one serious hot flash—or as I like to say, *power surge.*" She scoops up a tray of rocky road brownies before pausing to look at the seven-layer cake sitting pretty on a glass platter. "What talent you have.

It never ceases to amaze me. You really are something special, Lottie."

She blows me a kiss as she speeds right past me.

I suppose I do have a talent, and I'm not talking about my expertise in the kitchen. I have a supernatural knack that is quickly morphing into a curse. Not only did I *see*, and *hear* the bear—I witnessed the fact he was able to upturn those cookie sheets.

Never before has that happened. Never before has it gone this far.

A bear of all creatures!

Never before has it been this dangerous.

I'm willing to bet someone in this very B&B is about to take their final breath.

One thing is clear: death has come to Honey Hollow once again.

Pick up Seven-Layer Slayer (Murder in the Mix 5) and read the rest NOW!

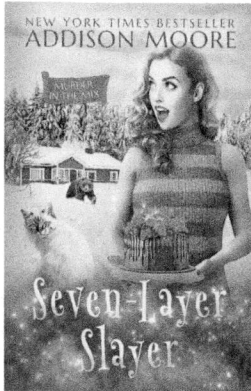

For up to the minute pre-order and new release alerts

*Be sure to **subscribe to Addison's mailing list** for sneak peeks and updates on all upcoming releases!
Or click over to the WEBSITE

✦Follow Addison on Amazon for the latest updates!

✦Follow Addison on **Bookbub!**
✦Like on **Facebook**

*Want to chat about the books? Hop over to Addison's Reader Corner on Facebook!

RECIPE

Gingerbread Cookies

From the kitchen of the Cutie Pie Bakery and Cakery

*I*t's Christmastime in Honey Hollow! And have I ever been baking up a storm. One of my best sellers this time of year are my gingerbread cookies and gingerbread houses. What's not to love about some yummy boys and girls and the cute little cottage they like to call home? The bakery even hosts gingerbread house decorating classes for both young and old alike. This recipe below is tried and true. It yields about 3 dozen cookies but I always double it if I'm making these at home. I hope you love them as much as the fine folks of Honey Hollow do! Happy Christmas baking!

*Note: You'll need to refrigerate this dough before baking for a minimum of 2 hours (or you can leave it there overnight).

Ingredients

4 cups sifted all-purpose flour (a little extra for rolling dough)
1 cup vegetable shortening
1 cup packed light brown sugar
1 cup light molasses
1 large egg (slightly whisked)
1 tablespoon baking soda
2 teaspoons baking powder
¼   teaspoon salt
1 tablespoon ground ginger
½ teaspoon ground cinnamon
½ teaspoon ground cloves
¼ cup cold water

Ingredients for royal icing

1 ½ cups powdered sugar
3-4 tablespoons milk

Directions

In a saucepan toss in molasses, brown sugar, and shortening. Cook over a medium heat until smooth and melted. Turn off stove and move saucepan to a cool burner. Add in ¼ cup cold water and baking soda, stir well and set to the side. Let cool to room temperature.

In a large mixing bowl or a stand mixer (I prefer the stand mixer), pour in the cooled ingredients from the saucepan. Add egg, baking powder, salt, cinnamon, ginger, and cloves. Stir well then add flour, 1 cup at a time mixing on medium (if you're using the stand mixer! And I hope you are. Your arms will feel this workout!) remove dough from mixer and shape and form into the shape of a ball. Cover with plastic wrap and refrigerate for at least 2 hours but to up 24 hours is fine too.

Preheat oven at 350° F

Line two cookie sheets with parchment paper. We're about to have some fun!

Toss some flour onto a work surface and roll out the dough ¼ of an inch. Use whatever gingerbread cookie cutter you like and cut out your cookies. Set you gingerbread men onto the cookie sheet about an inch apart. Bake 10 minutes. Decorate with icing (and whatever else your imagination can come up with. I've put sprinkles on my icing before to give it a festive flair).

These are great for holiday parties, cookie exchanges, or just to plain nibble on while curled up by a fire.

Whatever you do, don't let them run away. They're near impossible to catch. ;)

ACKNOWLEDGMENTS

Thank you so very much for hanging out in the MURDER IN THE MIX world once again! Lottie and her friends are super thankful you decided to come along for the ride. It's my pleasure to spend time in Honey Hollow, and I hope you feel the same!

Big thank you to Jodie Tarleton for taking the time to read the book. It is always a pleasure to work with you, girl! What more can I say? You're amazing!

To the fabulous Kaila Eileen Turingan-Ramos. You are such a huge blessing. Thank you for taking the time to scour the pages. You've got vision that defies understanding.

Thank you to the sweet and kind Shay Rivera for taking the time out of your busy schedule to read this manuscript. It is so very much appreciated! You are a sweetheart! And I mean that with all of my might.

A gigantic thank you to the wonderful Lisa Markson. There is none like you, and we both know it.

The biggest shout-out to the woman with all the answers and the most amazing eyes, Paige Maroney Smith. I love you forever. I'm so glad we're on this journey together!

And last, but never least, thank you to Him who sits on the throne. Worthy is the Lamb! Glory and honor and power are yours. I owe you everything, Jesus.

ABOUT THE AUTHOR

Addison Moore is a *New York Times, USA Today,* and *Wall Street Journal* bestselling author who writes contemporary and paranormal romance. Her work has been featured in *Cosmopolitan* Magazine. Previously she worked as a therapist on a locked psychiatric unit for nearly a decade. She resides on the West Coast with her husband, four wonderful children, and two dogs where she eats too much chocolate and stays up way too late. When she's not writing, she's reading. Addison's Celestra Series has been optioned for film by **20th Century Fox.**

f **y** **◎**

Printed in Great Britain
by Amazon

36363877R00118